Marriage & Murder
A Cedar Bay Cozy Mystery

BY

DIANNE HARMAN

Published by: Dianne Harman
www.dianneharman.com

Interior, cover design and website by
Vivek Rajan Vivek
www.vivekrajanvivek.com

ISBN: 978-1508465270

CONTENTS

ACKNOWLEDGMENTS

First of all, I want to thank all of my readers who have made this series so popular, I truly appreciate your taking the time and spending the money to read them. I always appreciate your thoughts about this book or any of my others. I'd love to hear from you. Here's my email address: dianne@dianneharman.com.

Secondly, I want to extend a special thanks to Vivek Rajan for the fabulous book covers he creates, his unending sound advice, and his taking the time to answer the gazillion questions I always have. I not only think of him as my editor, formatter, and marketing guru, I think of him as a friend and highly recommend him.

Finally, I want to thank my husband, Tom, for his support, belief in me, and love. Without him, none of this would be possible. And Tom, who knew we could have so much fun when we decided to retire! Thanks for the ride!!!

CHAPTER ONE

"Mom, how are you doing? Is there anything I can do to help?" Julia asked.

"Oh, sweetheart, I'm a nervous wreck. After your dad died, and while you and Cash were still very young, I never thought I'd marry anyone again. Yet here I am, and the wedding is less than twenty-four hours away. If you'd like to help me, you could call Jesse at The Crush and confirm that he'll be bringing the wine to the house after the ceremony tomorrow."

"It's already been done. Mike asked me to call him, and Jesse said he'd be here after the wedding to get set up. Amanda from Amanda's Flower Shop told me yesterday when I called her that she'd be delivering the flowers this afternoon for here at the house along with our wedding bouquets. The floral arrangements for the church will be delivered about nine tomorrow morning. I can't wait to see the spray of orchids she designed for you to carry. She told me she was going to make it with pink, lavender, and cream-colored baby orchids. I remember from when I was in high school and worked there, orchids were her favorite flowers, and I'll bet it will be spectacular. Given that tomorrow is Valentine's Day and probably her busiest day of the year, and add your wedding to that, I kind of feel sorry for her. What else do you need me to do?"

"At the moment, just keep me from falling apart."

1

"Mom, you'll do fine. At least you don't have to worry about keeping your coffee shop open and trying to run it and get married at the same time. It was really nice of Roxie and her friends to take over the operation of Kelly's Koffee Shop, so you could spend this week getting ready for your wedding. They're also going to help with the food at the reception, right?"

"Yes, they'll prepare all of it with one exception. We decided on a lot of appetizers, hot and cold, and instead of a wedding cake…"

"What do you mean instead of a wedding cake?" Julia asked, interrupting her.

"Well, at our age, having a miniature likeness of a groom dressed in a tuxedo and a bride dressed in a white gown with a long fancy train on the top of a tiered wedding cake, seemed kind of silly to me. Instead, I decided to have raspberry tarts, since we're getting married on Valentine's Day. I made them myself using an old family recipe from your grandmother Cora. It's really simple because the crust is made from cookie dough you buy at the store, although I can remember her making her own cookie dough and freezing it. That was before you could buy it at the store. I thought red raspberries would be a nice touch on Valentine's Day."

"When you put it that way, you're probably right. It's just that I've never been to a wedding where they didn't have a wedding cake with little roses and stuff."

"That may be true, but at your age, I'll bet you haven't attended too many second time around weddings."

"You're right. I'm so happy you found Mike. He's a wonderful man, and the two of you will make a beautiful couple. Cash really likes him too. The one thing Cash and I wish is that you'd stop trying to solve Mike's criminal cases. After all, he's the county sheriff, and it's up to him to solve cases when a crime has been committed. I know you've told me you just help him with his cases, but between you, Lady, and Rebel, sounds like a lot more than that is going on, and we're worried it might be dangerous for you."

"I suppose so, but all I do is try to help him, and I've never been in danger," she said, mentally crossing her fingers behind her back. "You know, it's pretty strange. I've lived my whole life in Cedar Bay and until last June, I'd never heard of a murder happening around this area, and now there have been three. Sure hope three's a lucky number, and that's the end of them."

Michelle continued, "I've always thought there was something magical about Cedar Bay, kind of Brigadoon-like. I don't know of anything that pleases me more than seeing the sun or the moon reflecting on the bay with the high cliffs surrounding it and the forests all around. I love Oregon and living in a small town. To me, it's the most beautiful place in the world, although admittedly, I haven't traveled the world, but I've never had a desire to. It seems like everything I've ever wanted is right here. Everybody knows almost everybody, and they're so friendly. No wonder we get so many tourists. Most of the houses are enchanting well-kept up early 20th century homes, the streets are canopied with trees, and the shops are simply charming. Plus, I think I must be the luckiest of all of them, having Kelly's Koffee Shop situated right on the pier that juts out into the bay. I never get tired of the smell of ocean air or the smell of the nearby forests. With the lushness of the forests surrounding the town, it's no wonder it started out as a lumber town. No, I'm definitely one of the luckiest people in the world to live right here in Cedar Bay."

"I feel the same way. Even though I live in San Francisco, part of me will always consider Cedar Bay home. Let's get back to the wedding. When are Roxie and her friends bringing the food to the house?"

"They're coming after the coffee shop closes, probably around three or four this afternoon. I thought of something you can do for me. You can transfer everything that's in the kitchen refrigerator out to the one in the garage. They're going to need all the space they can get in the kitchen refrigerator. Since I've got a little time until they get here, I'm going to set up the food table, and I'll have Mike and Cash set up the table for the wine and soft drinks when they get back."

"Speaking of Mike and Cash, I haven't seen them around for awhile. Where are they? Did Mike take Cash to his office?"

"No. Mike's taking a few days off. Cash was planning on wearing a suit he'd left here at the house when he gives me away tomorrow, but he's lost so much weight since he's been in Afghanistan, Mike decided they needed to pay a visit to Henry and have the suit taken in. When Mike told Henry the problem, he said he'd make it a top priority."

"Are you kidding me? Henry is still working? Good grief, he must be at least eighty years old."

"I'm sure he is. He comes to the coffee shop every day for lunch and has for as long as I can remember. He and Doc are the two people I can always count on being there at lunchtime."

"How's Doc doing? I remember you told me he was engaged to the town psychologist."

"Yes, and I couldn't be happier for them. I don't think you've met Liz, but you'll get a chance to meet her tomorrow."

"I'm glad I never needed to go to a psychologist when I lived here, but after Roger left me, I found a good one in San Francisco. Probably saved my life, and sure helped me get over feeling that I was worthless and deserved to have someone leave me."

"Oh, honey. I'm so sorry," Kelly said wrapping her arms around Julia and gently stroking her long black hair. "I didn't know it was that bad."

"There was no reason to worry you, particularly when you're a good day's drive away."

"Well, I'm glad you were smart enough to know you needed to get some help. How are you doing now?" she asked pushing Julia away and looking closely at her.

Good grief. She looks exactly like I looked at that age. Same black hair, same porcelain-like complexion, and a full figure. She even wears her hair swept up like I do. I just want her to be happy, and I'm glad Roger left her when he did. Would have been a lot harder after there were a couple of kids around.

"Mom, I'm doing fine," Julia said, stepping back and looking down at the ground. "Uh, there's something I probably should tell you. I suppose now is as good a time as any."

As soon as Julia uttered the words, Kelly felt sick to her stomach, and she was afraid Julia could hear her heart thudding in her chest. *Please, no problems just before the wedding, please.* "What should you tell me?"

"Well," Julia said, nervously twisting her watchband. "I've met someone I like a lot."

"Darling, that's wonderful. Tell me about him. Let's sit down for a minute. I need to take a break anyway."

"His name is Brad O'Hearn. He's a psychologist."

"Wait a minute, Julia. Is this the psychologist you've been seeing?"

"No, Mom. It's unethical to have that kind of a relationship with your therapist. Brad's office is across the hall from the woman I was seeing. We accidently met in the hall a number of times, and one day he asked me if I'd like to join him for coffee. I did, and we've been seeing each other for several months now."

"Julia, that's wonderful! I'm so happy for you."

"There's a little more to the story. He was previously married and unbeknownst to him, his wife had started using cocaine. She overdosed one day and died, leaving him with two children. Now he's a single parent raising his two daughters who are three and five."

"Oh, those poor little girls! How serious are you two?"

"Serious enough I'm thinking of moving in with him."

"I see. How do you get along with his daughters?"

"They like me, so that's not a problem." She paused and looked out the large bay window that provided a scenic view of Cedar Bay with the sun shining on its smooth blue surface.

"I'm not a big fan of people moving in together, but I'm also not much of an example considering Mike and I have been living together for several months," Kelly said, "but I have to say in our defense that Mike did ask you and Cash for permission to marry me. He moved in after that."

"Mom, my generation is a little different. It's not that big of a deal."

"It might be a big deal to those two little girls if you got close to them and then moved out, and they lost another mommy."

"That's not going to happen. The day before I came up here Brad asked me to marry him, and I said yes. We haven't gotten the ring yet or set the date, but I am going to marry him."

"Julia, I'm really happy for you, but I sense there's more to this. What are you not telling me?"

"Mom," she said, tears welling up in the corner of her large brown eyes, "Brad's afraid he's not the father of the girls. A friend of his ex-wife's visited him after his wife died and told Brad that his ex-wife had a lot of affairs, and that the girls probably weren't his."

"She told him that, and she called herself a friend?"

"Brad thinks she's as addicted to coke as his wife was."

"Did he know his wife was hooked on cocaine?"

"He knew she'd used drugs in the past and had even been in rehab for a while, but she swore when she met him she was drug-free, and her drug use had been nothing more than what everyone else was doing at that time. According to Brad, there was never anything in her behavior to indicate otherwise, but evidently she'd relapsed. She was with her friend the afternoon she died. This whole issue of whether or not he's the father of the girls is tearing him apart."

"I can see where it would. Let me talk to Mike about it. Maybe there's some way to find out. I kind of remember he did something with DNA in one of his investigations. As much as I'd love to keep talking to you, I see Amanda's van coming up the street. I imagine Roxie and her friends won't be far behind. Julia, I'm so happy for you! Well, look at it this way; even if the girls aren't Brad's, he's still the only daddy they've ever known. If he'd adopted two little girls, I'm sure he'd love them and wouldn't care who their biological father was. So what's the difference?"

"I'd never thought about it quite like that. I think that kind of logic will appeal to Brad and make him feel a lot better. Mom, maybe you should have been a psychologist."

"Fraid not, sweetheart. It's just comes from years of being the owner of Kelly's Koffee Shop and having everyone tell me their problems. I'm kind of like a bartender. Now off to refrigerator duty!"

I wish Julia had waited until after the wedding to tell me about Brad's fear of not being the father of the little girls. I don't have a good feeling about this.

CHAPTER TWO

Valentine's Day dawned with the sun gently shining on Cedar Bay, more like a typical summer day in Southern California and totally unusual for a February day in Oregon.

"Mom," Julia said as they sipped their coffee, "Want to share what you're thinking about this morning?"

"It's kind of hard to believe the big day is finally here. Mike and I decided in November that we'd get married today, and between the holidays and Scott's murder at the White Cloud Retreat Center, so much has happened it seems like it's been no time at all."

"I was sorry to hear about Scott's death. I went to a yoga class once with you and met him. Even though he was a Zen Master, he sure seemed like a down-to-earth person."

"He was. To change the subject, I've only got a couple of hours before Cash comes to the house to pick us up. I better start thinking about getting dressed. By the way, Mike, Cash, and Doc decided to spend the night out at Doc's ranchette and have sort of a mini bachelor party since Doc's going to be Mike's best man at the wedding. It was really nice of him to host it. It's kind of strange, but I was the one who suggested to Mike that it might be a fun thing for the three of them to do. If I'm going to be ready in time, think I better shift into high gear."

"Mom, let's be honest," Julie said, grinning broadly. "You just didn't want Mike to see you on your wedding day before you walked down the aisle, did you? That's kind of cute."

"Yeah, I know it's kind of schmaltzy, but in today's world, it's probably wise to take every precaution you can, so you don't have problems later on."

"Well, schmaltzy or not, I think it's utterly adorable. Now let's turn you into a beautiful bride-to-be."

Promptly at 9:30 Cash walked through the front door. "Mom, Julia," he said in a loud voice, "it's time for the big show. I just dropped Mike and Doc off at the church and Father Brown's already there. From the number of cars in St. Patrick's parking lot, I think the church is going to be full."

"You're kidding, right?" Kelly asked. "The wedding isn't until 10:00."

"No, I am definitely not kidding. Everybody around here has been in Kelly's Koffee Shop at one time or another, and everybody knows the county sheriff. This is probably the county's wedding of the century. You may have a lot of people at the wedding who weren't even invited."

"Bite your tongue. It never occurred to me that people would just show up if they hadn't been invited. That's pretty tacky."

"Tacky or not, from the looks of things in the parking lot I think it's going to happen. I may have to let you both off at the back door of the church and then try and find a parking place. Ready?" he said, holding out his arms to both of them. Julia and Kelly each put their arm through his and walked out the door to the waiting car. The three of them made an attractive trio; a slender muscular man with a military haircut and a lovely young woman who looked very much like the beautiful older woman beside her.

"Mom, this is exactly what I was afraid of," Cash said, as he pulled the car around to the back of the church, "I'll let you out here, and I'll be back after I park the car. Hate to tell you this, but it already looks like it's standing room only in St. Pat's."

Kelly visibly paled, as he spoke. "Mom, it'll work out," Julia said. "You have Cash, me, Mike, and Doc. You'll be fine. Remember, everyone is just happy for both of you, and that's why they're here."

"We should have eloped," Kelly said with a look of resignation in her eyes.

"Kelly, Julia, I'm glad you're here," Father Brown said, greeting them, as they entered the church. "Please follow me. There's a long private corridor we can use to get to the front of the church and avoid everyone. Cash is going to meet us there, so he can walk you down the aisle. I do have one question I have to ask you. Why did you invite so many people? Surely, you must know that St. Patrick's can't seat this many people."

"I only invited one hundred people, Father. The rest of the people weren't sent an invitation."

"Well, we'll make do, and just consider it a huge compliment to you and Mike. In all the years of my time conducting weddings here at St. Patrick's, nothing like this has ever happened. Here we are. You can wait in this little ante room, and remain out of sight until the music starts. I'm going back now, but I'll meet you in front of the altar where Mike will be waiting for you to come down the aisle. The two of you have about ten minutes until we begin."

"Mom, I have the ring you're giving to Mike, and here's the box with your bouquet of orchids."

Kelly took the box from her and opened it. "Oh my gosh! That's the most beautiful thing I've ever seen. Amanda really outdid herself," she said, looking at the spray of delicate pink, lavender, and cream-colored orchids mixed with baby's breath. "I told her I'd be wearing a cream-colored dress, and this bouquet will be perfect with it."

"Well, it's a good thing you're getting married today and not in the fifteenth century."

"Why?" Kelly asked, taking her eyes off of her wedding bouquet and looking at Julia.

"Because I read once that people who lived in the fifteenth century only took one bath a year and that was in May, so everyone got married in June, but they always carried flowers hoping the scent of the flowers would freshen the air, because it had been a month since their bath, and they were a little worried they might smell. That's how the whole carrying flowers thing started."

"Julia, that's the most disgusting thing I've ever heard," Kelly said, laughing. "Where did you come up with that, and why would you even remember it?"

"I don't know," Julia said. "It's probably what makes me good at crossword puzzles and Jeopardy. The shrink I was seeing told me I have what's called an eidetic memory. I can remember all kinds of things, like what I was wearing when I had a conversation with someone, or what I was doing before I talked to them. All kinds of things no one else ever remembers. She told me that kind of memory is unusual in children, but it's almost unheard of in adults. Guess that makes me special. You should be proud of me!"

"You know I'm proud of you, but you must have gotten that from your father. I certainly don't have a memory like that."

The door opened, and Cash walked in. "Sorry, Mom, but I had trouble finding a place to park. I was about ready to go back to the house, leave the car in the driveway, and just walk over. Where did all these people come from?"

"I have no idea. Uh-oh, I hear music. Is that our cue?"

"Almost. Father Brown said we should get ready to walk down the aisle when we heard the first song. There will be a slight pause, and then it's show time. Julia goes first, and you and I will follow her.

Are you okay?" he said noticing the tears that were starting to well up in her eyes.

"Mother, please don't cry" Julia said. "I repeat, do not cry. Your makeup will spread all over your face, and you'll look like a clown in the wedding photos." Julia quickly dabbed at the corners of Kelly's eyes with a tissue and said, "Cash did not come all the way from Afghanistan to escort a sobbing woman down the aisle. Am I making myself perfectly clear?"

"Yes. I'm fine now." She turned to Cash. "Sounds like it's time, honey. Let's do it."

He opened the door and Julia, her mother's maid of honor, began to walk down the aisle towards Doc and Mike, who were both smiling broadly. Kelly and Cash followed her. Every eye in the church was on the handsome young man and the beautiful older woman.

Kelly smiled lovingly at Mike and Doc and then noticed that Mike was wiping his eyes. She couldn't believe what she was seeing. It was completely out of character for the attractive middle aged man who wore the mantle of the power of his office as sheriff as if it was a second skin. She realized she'd never seen Mike cry or even come close to it.

Whatever god that's out there and is in charge of crying, please listen up. I can't cry. I don't care if Mike and everyone else is crying, I can't. Julia's right. I'll look like a mess. I promise to never tell a white lie to Mike again if you can get me through this without crying. Honest.

The ceremony was beautiful and while almost everyone in the audience was quietly or openly weeping with joy and happiness for the couple, the bride remained free from tears. Evidently the gods had listened to her urgent plea.

Kelly and Mike had opted for a celebration of marriage which didn't include Mass, because he wasn't Catholic. Given the fact it was a second marriage, and that he was divorced, even though his ex-wife was now deceased, Father Brown thought it would be a good idea to not have Mass at the wedding. It seemed like only a few minutes had gone by when Father Brown said, "You may now kiss the bride," and Mike did, heartily, to the amusement of everyone in the church. At the conclusion of the ceremony, Mike and Kelly, along with Doc, Julia, and Cash walked up the aisle. In an unheard of deviance from the norm, as the five of them made their way to the rear of the church, the well-wishers broke out in applause and whistles. Clearly, the couple was well-loved by all of the people in the church. Phil, the town photographer, hoped they'd keep smiling like that for the photographs that were to follow the ceremony.

*****

"Mike, if all those people who were at the wedding come to the house, we're in trouble," Kelly said as Cash drove them home from St. Patrick's. "There's not enough food, and I told Jesse to only plan on about one hundred people. I also told him a lot of them probably wouldn't have any wine. I don't know what to do."

"You're not going to do anything. We're going to enjoy the reception, and if they're rude enough to show up when they weren't invited, they just won't get anything to eat or drink," he said, bringing her hand up to his lips and kissing it. "Nothing is going to ruin this day, okay?"

"Yes, but…"

"No. No buts. This is not our problem. We're going to enjoy the afternoon with friends and family, and that's it. Do we have a deal?"

"Deal," Kelly said.

Cash turned and gave Mike a thumbs up. "Glad someone can get her attention. I was never very good at it."

"Wish I could say she was this amenable all the time."

"Hey guys, it's my wedding day," Kelly said, laughing. "That's enough."

When they got back to the house, Jesse's big white refrigerated truck with the words "The Crush" prominently displayed in large letters on the side was already in the driveway. He'd left directly after the service while the wedding party had to remain for photographs. Roxie and her two friends were in the kitchen, setting up. They had opted to miss the wedding, so they could get ready for the reception.

"How's everything going, Roxie?" Kelly asked.

"We're fine. Just need some people, but from what I heard from Jesse, that's not going to be a problem. He said the church was ready to split apart from the number of people who were there. I thought you limited the guest list to one hundred."

"I did. I don't know where they came from, and I hope they don't come here."

"They won't. They were probably just happy to see the two of you get married and wanted to share your joyous day. By the way, since I missed the wedding in order to get this reception set up, and you know how I love photography, I claim first look at Phil's photos after you get them from him."

"That's a promise, and Roxie, thanks for everything."

Jesse stood behind the large table that had been set up for wine and soft drinks. White wines were chilling in glass ice buckets, the red wines had been opened so they could breathe, and there was an ice chest filled with Pellegrino, soft drinks, and water behind the table. Kelly looked over at him, surprised to see that he was sweating and seemed to be on edge.

Wonder what's up with Jesse? She thought. *I've never seen him look anything but unflappable.*

Mike clapped his hands in order to get everyone's attention. "Would everyone please come over to where Jesse is?" Kelly, Roxie, her two friends, Doc, Cash, Julia, and Liz, Doc's fiancée, joined Mike and Jesse. "Jesse, would you open the two bottles of champagne I asked you to bring?"

"Mike, we didn't say anything about champagne," Kelly said, looking confused.

"I want to propose a toast before the guests arrive. Jesse, would you hand everyone a glass?" A few moments later he said, "To Kelly, without whom my life would have been meaningless. You fill my soul in a way that nothing else ever has or ever will, and I've never been happier than at this moment. I love you. Please, everyone, raise your glasses to Kelly, the woman of my dreams."

Julia turned to Kelly and whispered, "Mom, don't even think about letting those tears spill down your cheeks. I guess I have one job to do today and that's keeping you from crying and making a mess of yourself." Once again she wiped away the tears gathering in the corners of Kelly's eyes.

Cash walked over to Mike. "Julia and I want to welcome you into our family. There's no one we'd rather see Mom with. We're really happy for both of you and if you don't mind, from now on I'd like to call you Dad."

Mike put his arm around Cash and hugged him. "Thank you and I promise I'll do my best to make her happy."

Cash grinned at him. "I have no doubt of that, but if you don't, let's put it this way. I carry a gun, too, and I've probably had a little more combat training than you have, plus I'm about twenty-five years younger than you are. I don't mean this in a mean way, but the extra twenty-five pounds that you're carrying may not be all muscle. I wasn't exactly sitting at a desk in Iraq, and I sure haven't been in Afghanistan."

Kelly stepped over and hugged both of them. "Cash, I appreciate your trying to take care of me, but I'm a big girl now!" she said smiling at both of them. The moment was broken as the doorbell rang, and within minutes the house was filled with well-wishers. Three hours later Kelly and Mike had lost track of the number of people who had come to eat, drink, and celebrate in their house that overlooked Cedar Bay.

When Kelly had said good-bye to the last guest, she closed the door, slumped against it and said, "We're out of food, we're out of drinks, and I'm out of smiles. If I'm exhausted, all of you must be too. I can't thank you enough for making this one of the happiest days of my life."

"Wait a minute," Mike said, "only one of the happiest?"

"I've had a few other peak moments in my life, like when I gave birth to these two wonderful people," she said, motioning towards Cash and Julia. "Don't push your luck, Sheriff Mike. Anyway, again, thank you all for everything."

Jesse left a few moments later. The only things he had to take back to The Crush were the glasses, coolers, and ice chests. Everything else had been consumed by the thirsty celebrating guests, invited and uninvited. The clean-up in the kitchen was just as minimal. Everything had been eaten, so the only thing that had to be done was to wash the serving dishes.

"Mom, I think all four of us are exhausted," Cash said. "I'd planned on cooking a nice wedding dinner for you two on my last night here in the States, but I think we're all too tired to enjoy it. Would it be okay with the three of you if we change clothes, and I'll just make some sandwiches instead?"

"Sweetheart, right now that sounds like the best wedding dinner I could possibly have. Okay with you, Mike?"

"Absolutely. See how easy I'm going to be?"

"Right," Kelly said, rolling her eyes.

CHAPTER THREE

Early the next morning found all four of them standing next to Julia's bright red Nissan. Kelly, with tears shining in her eyes, said, "Thank you both so much for taking part in our wedding and spending the week with us. I know I speak for Mike as well as myself when I say how much both of us loved having you, and you know you're always welcome. I may be married to him, but please consider this to be your second home."

"Mom, Mike, congratulations again! It was a wonderful wedding, but I'm sure you're both glad it's over, and your lives can get back to normal. Cash, are you ready? I've got to get you to the San Francisco airport for the first leg of your trip back to Afghanistan, and we've got a long drive ahead of us," Julia said, getting into the Nissan.

"Cash, I know I sound like an overanxious mother, but I worry so much about you. Please be safe. How much longer do you think you'll be stationed there?" Kelly asked, chewing on her lower lip, a sign Mike knew meant she was really nervous.

"Don't worry about me, Mom, I'm very careful. I only have a few more months to go, so I'll be even extra careful." He looked at Julia who was drumming her fingers on the steering wheel. "Okay, I recognize that gesture from when we were kids. Time to go. Love you both!" He got in the car, and they both waved as Julia backed the car out of the driveway and headed south to San Francisco.

Mike put his arm around Kelly when they got back in the house and said, "Sweetheart, try not to worry. I've told you before that he's street smart, and in that war zone it counts a lot more than a fancy law degree from Harvard."

"I know, it's just...just." Tears slid down her cheeks. "I'm so worried about him. I still don't even understand why we're over there."

Mike held her close. "You're not the only one. All we can do is pray for his safe return, and I predict it will be a safe return. To change the subject, Mrs. Reynolds, since it's Sunday, and you don't have to work today, now that your children are gone, I think it might be nice to take a little time and to properly consummate our marriage. Would that be acceptable to you?"

"Absolutely, Sheriff Mike. Thought you'd never ask." She turned to the dogs. "Rebel, Lady, stay," she said, walking arm and arm down the hall with Mike.

*****

A few hours later, when they were finished with their honeymoon breakfast, Mike said, "I'd like to go over to The Crush and thank Jesse again for bringing all of the wine and soft drinks, not to mention the glasses. Want to come with me?"

"Absolutely. He did a wonderful job for us. Let's take the dogs. I kenneled them most of the day yesterday, and they're probably chomping at the bit to go somewhere. Why don't you get ready, and I'll do the dishes, but don't get too used to it!"

"Deal. I'll do them tonight."

"Deal."

While she was doing the dishes, she remembered she hadn't told Mike about Julia and the new man in her life, Brad. When Mike returned to the kitchen, she filled him on Julia's engagement to Brad and his worry regarding his daughters.

"I've been thinking about their situation while I was doing the dishes. Isn't there something about a DNA match that would positively determine whether Brad is the father of the girls? I seem to remember seeing some show on television that said it could absolutely be determined with a DNA test whether or not someone was the parent of a particular child. I've heard it takes an incredibly long time for most people to get the test results, but I was thinking, since you're a sheriff, couldn't you get it done faster?"

"Yes, I probably could, but are you sure you want to get involved? I'm not sure I do."

"What do you mean?"

"What if I was able to fast track the test and get the results? What if it turned out Brad wasn't the father of the two little girls? What would happen to the relationship between Julia and Brad on the one hand, and my relationship with both of them, on the other hand, if I was the one who told her he wasn't the father?"

"I see where you're going, Mike. Maybe we should tell Julia what we're thinking and ask her if she'd like your help in getting a DNA test. If she decides she wants to do it, she'll have to live with the results, but if it turns out he's not their father…"

"You mentioned something about Julia needing to see a psychologist after Roger left her. Do you think she's emotionally stable enough to withstand someone else leaving her? I mean, we don't know what Brad will do if he finds out he isn't the father. Don't forget, neither one of us has even met him. The only thing you know about him is what Julia has told you."

"I really don't know. After your kids get to be a certain age, you only know as much about them as they're willing to tell you, so in answer to your question, no, I don't know if she could emotionally hold up if Brad left her. I'll think about it, and we can talk later."

"Let me know what you decide, but I have to tell you my initial reaction is to stay out of it. Okay, time to go see Jesse. The Crush should be open by now. Rebel, Lady, car," he said.

The dogs ran out to the car, waiting patiently for someone to open the door for them. They hopped in the backseat and sat down, ready for their next adventure.

CHAPTER FOUR

When they drove past the front of The Crush, Kelly said, "No matter how many times I drive by Jesse's shop, it always makes me happy. I mean look at the color of that awning, how perfect is purple for a place that sells wine? No wonder people love his shop."

Mike pulled his patrol car into the parking lot behind The Crush and said, "Looks like the back door's open. Jesse must have just gotten here." He parked the car, got out, and then opened the back door to let the dogs out. Kelly opened the car door on her side and got out as well.

Suddenly Rebel ran over to the back door of The Crush and stopped, standing stone still with his hackles raised and looking through the open door into the interior of the store. Lady was standing right behind him. He turned his head around as if to say to the little yellow lab, "Don't go any farther. Stay where you are."

"What's going on?" Mike said. "What are you two dogs doing?" Kelly walked up next to Mike and started to enter the store. Rebel blocked the door. "Rebel, move!" Rebel didn't budge.

Mike turned to Kelly and asked, "How do you get this ninety pound dog that's made of steel to move?"

"Been my experience, you can't. And if he's stopping us from going in The Crush, we better see if there's a problem. Why don't you just step over him?"

As Mike stepped over him, Rebel began growling, followed by Lady. Both dogs seemed deeply agitated, and their deep growling quickly increased in intensity. Kelly tried to step over Rebel, but he was too big. As soon as Mike walked through the door, he stopped and looked down at the floor.

"What's wrong?" she asked. "Is everything okay?"

"No. Everything is definitely not okay. Jesse's been shot, and I'm sure he's dead."

"Oh no! I'm coming in." She firmly put her hand on Rebel, and the two of them walked through the open door, followed by Lady whose growling had turned to yips. The dogs smelled the blood that had pooled around Jesse's still form where he lay on the floor, a large bullet hole clearly visible in his chest. Kelly's legs started to buckle under her, and she felt faint. She knelt on the floor and began to sob uncontrollably, tears rolling down her cheeks. She vaguely heard Mike's voice and made out the words, "Murder, Jesse, The Crush," as he spoke into his phone. Moments later she felt his strong hands lift her up and guide her to a nearby chair. "Take it easy, sweetheart. Put your head between your legs, and breathe deeply. You'll feel better in a minute or two. Rich and some of my other deputies will be here shortly. Rebel, Lady, stay with Kelly. Stay."

The two dogs obediently went over and stood next to Kelly, trying to protect her from whatever it was that was threatening her, although there was nothing they could do about the sadness she felt engulfing her.

The sound of sirens filled the parking lot within minutes as several sheriffs' cars skidded to a stop behind The Crush. Car doors slammed shut, and heavy footsteps kicked gravel up from the parking lot as a number of uniformed deputies rushed from their cars and came through the open door. The room was soon filled with the men and women whose job it is to do the police work that always needs to be done at the scene of a crime, especially if the crime is murder.

"Rich, secure the entire building and parking lot as an active crime scene. No one goes in or out without approval from either you or me. Jeff, Nita, you two know what to do. Get every bit of DNA evidence you can. Dust every surface for prints. This one's personal." He turned to Kelly, "We may have just had one of the shortest honeymoons on record. One of my men will drive you and the dogs back to the house. I don't know when I'll be home."

A short time later, the country coroner pulled up behind The Crush. He had to physically move his large belly away from the steering wheel in order to get out of his car. "Mike, I was right in the middle of Sunday brunch with the family. Some really good fried chicken and mashed potatoes with gravy," he said, licking his lips, his heavy jowls wagging. "Just had my first bite when I got your call. Dang, I wish killers would for once at least wait until I was through eating before they decide to kill somebody."

"I rather doubt whoever did this was worrying much about the coroner having to be called away from his special Sunday brunch," Mike retorted sarcastically. "Would have saved you the trouble of coming, but as you know, it's state policy. The county coroner has to examine the body to confirm that the victim is dead. Seems kind of stupid in this case. It's pretty obvious. One quick look at poor old Jesse is enough to know he's dead."

Mike stood beside the coroner as he quickly examined Jesse. "Well, what do you think?"

"I think he was killed within the hour. His body is still warm, and if he'd been dead for more than two hours rigor mortis would have started to set in, and it hasn't. Looks like he died from a gunshot to the chest. There's no exit wound, so when I do the autopsy, I'll be able to recover the bullet. I'll send it to the state police lab, and they'll have their ballistics expert determine the caliber. I'll tell them to give you a call when they know something. It will probably take a couple of days."

"Thanks, Leo. Sorry for interrupting your Sunday brunch. Since you're probably through here, you can have your assistant take the body to the morgue, and if you hurry you might even make it back home before dessert is served," Mike said. His words were met by a scowl from the overweight coroner who told his assistant he was through examining the body, and it should be taken to the morgue after Mike's men finished getting whatever evidence they could from it. He turned on his heel and waddled out to his car.

Mike spoke to one of his deputies who then walked over to where Kelly was seated and said, "Mrs. Reynolds, I can take you home now." Kelly stood up and gestured for Rebel and Lady to follow her. Rebel refused to move. "Rebel, come," she said. He stood rock solid still and looked in Mike's direction.

"Mike, Rebel wants to stay with you, and just like in the Humpty Dumpty nursery rhyme 'All the king's horses and all the king's men' aren't going to get him to move. As strong as he is, it would take all of your men to get him in the car. I think you and your deputies all have more important things to do at the moment, so just let him stay here with you. He probably feels he needs to be here to protect you."

"Okay. I'll take him with me when I leave." He walked over to her. "I know how much you liked Jesse and his family. I'm so sorry. When we finish here, I'll drive over and tell them the sad news."

"No. If you don't mind, I'd like to have your deputy take me to his mother's house, and I'll tell her now. It may be hours before your work here's finished, and I got to know the family pretty well when I took some food out to Jesse's father when he was terminally ill. Jesse was divorced and lived above The Crush. His mother and sister live only about a block away from here. I don't want them to hear about this from someone else, and you know how fast word travels in this little town of ours."

Kelly stepped through the rear door of The Crush, her heart heavy with grief. She'd only taken a few steps when she saw something glittering on the ground. She knelt down and picked it up, noticing that it was a small decorative pin with the Arabic numbers

"07" on it.

When this is over, she thought, *I'll do a little research and see if I can return it to its owner.* As she and Lady followed the young deputy to his patrol car, she slid the pin into a side pocket of her purse, intending to examine it later.

*****

Kelly rang the doorbell of Jesse's mother's well-kept modest two-story Queen Anne style home with white columns and a wrap-around porch. Seconds later a small white-haired older woman wearing a flowered apron opened the door. "Why, Kelly, how nice to see you. It's been a long time, dear. Please, come in," she said, giving Kelly a hug as she entered the hallway.

"Thank you, Mrs. Allen. I'm afraid I have some bad news. Why don't you sit down?"

"What's wrong? She asked, pushing her glasses up the ridge of her nose.

"Please, sit down. It's Jesse…"

Mrs. Allen interrupted her, "Has something happened to him? He was just here for lunch. I'm cleaning up the dishes right now."

Kelly put her hand on Mrs. Allen's arm and gently guided her into a chair that was next to where she was standing. "Yes, something has happened to him." She paused and took a deep breath. "Mrs. Allen, Jesse was murdered a little while ago. Sheriff Mike and I found his body at The Crush."

A large, plain-looking middle-aged woman suddenly ran shrieking into the room. Celia Parsons wore her grey hair cut in a short bob and wasn't wearing any make-up. "I just walked in through the back door and heard that. What are you talking about? My brother was here earlier. Momma called me over at the Historical Society and asked me to join them, but I couldn't get away because we were

25

having an important meeting. Why are you doing this to her?"

"Celia," Kelly said to the sour-faced stern-looking woman who had sat down in a chair next to her mother, "you know I wouldn't lie to you or your mother about something like this. Believe me, I would rather be just about anywhere else on earth right now, but I didn't want you to hear this terrible news from someone else."

"Tell me everything," Celia said, crossing her arms over her ample bosom and sinking back into her chair as if her gesture would negate whatever she was going to hear from Kelly in the next few minutes.

"All I know is that Mike and I drove to The Crush a little while after noon to personally thank Jesse for everything he did for us at the wedding reception yesterday. The back door was open, and we found Jesse lying on the floor. He'd been shot once in the chest and was dead."

At the word "dead," Mrs. Allen began rocking furiously back and forth and sobbing at the same time. Kelly could hear her mumble something that sounded like "It's not fair. First Herbert and now Jesse. The only two men in my life I ever loved. Who could do something like this?"

Celia got up from her chair, walked over to her mother, and put her arms around her. "Momma, we're going to be okay. I promise. I'm here with you. At least he didn't have to suffer from some disease like Daddy did. We'll be okay."

She turned and faced Kelly. "Does the sheriff have any idea who did it?"

"Not to my knowledge. No one was there when we arrived, and I didn't see anything that looked like a clue as to who might have killed him or why, but Mike and his staff may have found something by now. I just don't know."

"Well, for starters you might tell them to find out where Sophie Marchant was about lunchtime. Might be the first and probably the last person the sheriff would have to interview about Jesse's death. Wouldn't put anything past that French foreigner. I hate her."

"I'm sorry, but I don't know who you're talking about," Kelly said.

"Sure you do. She's that fancy-schmancy French woman who owns the big ugly house on the south side of Cedar Bay up on the cliff overlooking the bay, the one who wears expensive scarves and French perfume and has that soft voice and that stupid little French accent. She lives in Portland and uses the house on the weekends," she harrumphed.

"She was always going in The Crush asking my brother about this wine or that wine and could he recommend a good Oregon Pinot Noir, something that was comparable to a French Rhone. Makes me sick just thinking about her and her high falutin 'I'm better than you' attitude. That's one of the reasons why I'm president of the Historical Society. We're trying to preserve Cedar Bay and keep people like her and that monstrous modern looking glass house of hers out of our wonderful city. She never would have gotten permission to build that ugly house if I'd been president of the Historical Society at the time it was approved by the Planning Commission. Anyway, she was always mooning all over Jesse when she was in the store. It was disgusting."

Mrs. Allen had been listening in and following the conversation. "Celia, you know Jesse had strong feelings for her. Several times when you weren't around, he told me he was in love with her. He even said he was thinking of marrying her. She's not that bad. He brought her over to dinner once, and she was real nice to me."

"You're just saying that to protect Jesse. If you ask me, she's a classic example of a woman who has real loose morals, if you know what I mean," she said, raising her eyebrows. "All you have to do is look at her, and you know what I'm saying is the truth. Poor Jesse, he went for her line of garbage, hook, line and sinker. You know what those French women are like. I tell you she doesn't belong here in Cedar Bay."

"I really need to go now," Kelly said. "Would you like me to call Dr. Burkhart for you, Mrs. Allen? He could probably give you something to help you get through the next couple of days."

"No, Kelly. At my age, one becomes familiar with death. It's just that no mother should outlive her son. Somethin's not right about that. Goes against God's laws. I'll be okay. Don't you worry none. I've got Celia here, and with her love and support I'll get along."

"Here's my phone number if you need anything. I imagine Sheriff Mike will want to talk to both of you in a day or so. Again, I'm sorry to be the bearer of such bad news, but I didn't want you to hear it from someone else."

"Thank you," Celia said. "I think Momma needs to lie down for a little while, but mark my words, the sheriff needs to talk to Sophie Marchant before he wastes his time with anyone else. You tell him I said that."

"I will," Kelly said, opening the door and walking out to the waiting patrol car where Lady was standing in the front seat watching for Kelly's safe return. While she waved goodbye to Celia, she made a decision to try and find out if Sophie Marchant was staying at her big house on the cliff this weekend.

A few minutes later she said to the young deputy, "Thanks for the ride. You can just drop me off and go on back. I need to run a couple of errands anyway."

CHAPTER FIVE

Almost immediately after the deputy sheriff dropped Kelly off at her home, she and Lady got in her minivan and headed south from town. Five minutes later Kelly spotted a road that led off the highway and up to a large glass and wood house on the cliff overlooking Cedar Bay. She'd never met the owner of the house, Sophie Marchant, but she remembered a few years earlier how the town was buzzing about the large home that was being built overlooking the bay. She also vaguely remembered that there had been talk that it was too much house for a single woman, and the modern architectural style wasn't compatible with the majority of the homes in Cedar Bay, most of which had been built in the early years of the 20th century.

Kelly pulled into the circular driveway and parked. She walked up to the front door, noticing that she could easily see the bay and the ocean by looking through the expanse of glass on the front of the house which was repeated on the back side of the house. A red tile roof gave the house a distinct Mediterranean look which seemed out of place to Kelly, as the Oregon coast was almost always rainy and overcast. She rang the doorbell and the door was immediately opened by a beautiful 40ish looking woman dressed elegantly in a grey cashmere slack set with a maroon scarf casually thrown over her shoulder. Small pearl earrings and a matching necklace gleamed against her olive complexion and auburn ringlets.

"May I help you?" the woman asked.

"My name is Kelly Conner, oops, Kelly Reynolds, now. I was just married yesterday, and I'm not used to my new married name. My husband is the county sheriff."

"Yes, I've heard of you. You're the owner of Kelly's Koffee Shop, aren't you? I'm Sophie Marchant," she said, holding out her hand.

"Yes, that's who I am. May I come in? I'd like to talk to you for a few moments."

"Please. I see a dog in the front seat of your van that seems to be watching everything you do. Would you like to bring him with you?"

"If you don't mind, yes, and it's a her."

She returned to her minivan to get Lady, and the two of them walked into the house.

"What a beautiful little girl," Sophie said, holding out her hand so Lady could sniff it. "Would you mind if I give her a treat? I have a dog of my own, so I always keep treats on hand. Unfortunately I had to leave Amelie in Portland this weekend."

"Of course. I'm sure Lady would love it. Thank you very much. I'm afraid I have some bad news for you. I understand that you were acquainted with Jesse Allen, the owner of The Crush."

Sophie jerked her head up from where she'd been giving a treat to Lady. "Has something happened to Jesse?" she asked in a soft voice with a heavy French accent.

"Yes. My husband and I discovered his body earlier today. He'd been killed, apparently the victim of a vicious murder."

"*Mon Dieu. Non.* I don't believe it." Tears began to stream down her cheeks. "What monster could possibly do this? Why would someone do this? Did you know we were thinking of getting married? *Mon Dieu.*"

"I am so sorry. I'm a friend of Mrs. Allen's, and I didn't want her to hear about her son's death from the town gossips, so I went to her home a little while ago and told her. That's when she mentioned that you and Jesse were quite close. I thought it might be better for you if I came to your home and told you personally rather than getting a call from some stranger or seeing it on television."

Sophie sat down on one of the cream-colored couches in the large room that overlooked the bay and the late afternoon incoming fog which soon would reach land. She struggled to keep her composure and began to speak in her accented soft voice, "I met Jesse when I first came to Cedar Bay. I usually brought my own wine with me when I drove down from Portland, but the weekend I met him I had forgotten to pack it, and I do enjoy a good wine, so I stopped at The Crush to buy a nice bottle. There was an immediate attraction between the two of us, and from then on, whenever I came down for the weekend we would get together. We began to really care for one another. I'm divorced, and he's divorced. Neither of us has children. The only problem we had was his ex-wife. I never met her, but from what Jesse told me she wanted them to reconcile, and she was extremely jealous of anyone she thought might be interested in him. Evidently she said a lot of bad things about me, although I've never met her."

"I'm surprised he told his ex-wife about you," Kelly said.

"I don't think he did. I understand his ex-wife and his sister, Celia, remained good friends after the divorce, and I believe Celia was the one who told her about me."

"Knowing Celia, that doesn't surprise me. I'm sure my husband will want to talk to you about where you were around noon today. He'll probably be here tomorrow."

"I'm leaving for Portland tomorrow morning, so if he wants to talk to me he'll have to do it before I leave. Now that this has happened, I'm not sure I even want to come here anymore. Jesse was everything I ever hoped to find. Without him…" she stopped speaking in mid-sentence, sobbing uncontrollably.

Kelly got up from the couch and walked down the hall, trying to find a bathroom and some tissues. *Good grief. This has to be the most beautiful home I've ever been in. I don't know anything about art, but these paintings look like the real deal to me. And those glass sculptures in that display case next to the front door are stunning. I remember seeing some French art glass pieces in a magazine that were beautiful, and these are every bit as beautiful. Everywhere I look there's an incredible painting or art object. Wonder where all her money comes from. Ex-husband? Probably need to look her up on the Internet.*

She returned from the bathroom with several tissues and handed them to Sophie. "Again, Sophie, I'm so sorry to be the one to bring you this sad news. Is there anything I can do for you?"

"All I want to do is get out of here. Everywhere I look I see something that reminds me of him. I don't know if you're aware that Jesse had a master's degree in art history. He was torn between working in the world of art or in the world of wine. His father insisted he pursue a career in wine sales since so many new vineyards were being opened here in Oregon. He told me his father had been a very good father to him, and I think that's why he decided to open The Crush rather than go into art as a career."

"Well, you just never know about people. And you, what is your background, if you don't mind me asking?"

"I worked in a fashion house in Paris and met my ex-husband through friends. He was the managing partner of an international banking company that sent him to the United States, actually to Portland, to head up the growing office there. His family owned the largest perfume company in France, but he chose to work in banking instead of going into the family business. We were married for ten years when he decided that women who worked in the movie industry were more interesting than I was. He'd been traveling back and forth between Los Angeles and Portland. He met a starlet, divorced me, and married her. He managed to immediately get transferred to the Los Angeles headquarters of the banking company. It may have been guilt money, but I received a very large settlement from him, as you can see," Sophie said, gesturing broadly at the surrounding house and its contents.

"Yes, this house is simply beautiful. You have excellent taste."

"*Non*. Many of the things were chosen by Jesse. We used to spend a lot of our time together looking at auction catalogs. He was very knowledgeable about French art glass. The Daum and Lalique works in the cabinet near the front door were chosen by him. *Mon Dieu*, I'm going to miss him so much," she said, starting again to softly cry.

"I'm so sorry. Would you like me to call someone for you?"

"*Non*. Thank you. I want to be alone. I'll leave tomorrow morning, and I don't think I'll be back. I can have someone come and pack up the things in the house. Thank you, Kelly, for coming and telling me. I know it must have been hard," she said, standing up and walking to the front door with Kelly.

"Not as hard as it is for you. Here's my business card if you need anything and oh, would you write your telephone number on this one, so I can give it to Mike? As I said, I'm sure he's going to want to talk to you. Again, I'm sorry."

Kelly took the card from Sophie and then spontaneously put her arms around her and hugged her gently. "I'm sorry we didn't meet before. I would have liked to have gotten to know you. Please feel free to call me. I hope we meet again."

"You are very kind, *mon amie*, thank you."

Kelly and Lady got in her minivan and drove back down the road to the highway. *Poor thing. How hard it must be to find love, to have a second chance, and then, in the blink of an eye, lose it. I really feel for her, and I meant it when I said I wished we'd met earlier. I like her. I don't know why Celia hates her so much. Maybe Jesse's ex-wife poisoned the well and made Sophie out as a bad person.*

"Lady, time to go home. It's been quite a weekend and tomorrow we have to get back to work."

CHAPTER SIX

The next morning it was still dark when Kelly woke up. She looked over at Mike, her husband of two days and still couldn't believe they were married. Even more, she couldn't believe that less than a day after their marriage they'd discovered Jesse Allen's body in his wine shop.

I remember an old saying that went something like, "from the sublime to the ridiculous," but yesterday was more like, "from being ecstatic to being devastated." I can't imagine who would want Jesse dead. Wonder if Mike found out anything, but I don't want to wake him. I looked at the clock when he came to bed last night, and it was after midnight. It's only 5:30 now, and he needs more sleep than that. I'll have to wait to find out.

She gestured to Rebel and Lady to follow her to the kitchen. She let them out into the back yard while she made a cup of coffee. After she was dressed in jeans and a tee-shirt, she looked over at Mike, silently saying goodbye, and that she'd see him later in the day. While she was looking at him, she noticed Rebel had gotten up on the king-size bed and was lying next to Mike, sound asleep.

Good grief. Rebel's never done that before. Mike must let him get in bed with him after I've left for the coffee shop. So much for training the dogs to stay off the furniture. Oh well, a wise woman I know once told me to choose my battles wisely. Guess this is one I'll let go.

She and Lady walked out to her minivan, and once they were inside, she turned to the growing puppy that was sitting in the back seat and said, "Lady, don't even think about it. You are not to get on the bed. We'll pretend we didn't see that. Deal?" She could swear that Lady nodded her head in agreement.

In just a few minutes they arrived at the parking lot next to the pier where Kelly's Koffee Shop was located. She and her late husband had taken it over from her parents when they retired and moved to the Phoenix area. She got out of the van and stood for a moment looking at the coffee shop. Memories of her grandmother teaching her to cook when Kelly was a little girl, her husband, Mark, who had died at an early age from a rare form of cancer, the lumbermen who used to patronize the coffee shop when the lumber business was good, were just a few of the fleeting thoughts that swept through her mind as she gazed at it.

She knew a lot of people wouldn't be able to understand how someone could love a coffee shop, but she did. It had been a lifesaver for her when Mark died, and provided her with the means to support herself and her two children. She particularly loved the people she'd hired and considered to be an extended family. There was Roxie, who had been with her for over ten years, and was everyone's favorite waitress. Charlie, the son of Chief Many Trees, was the best short order cook who had ever worked in the coffee shop. Although he could be short-tempered when it came to issues regarding Native Americans and how he thought the government had ruined them, he never let it interfere with his work at the coffee shop. Madison was a relatively new addition to the staff and would soon be leaving to work at Wanda's Beauty Salon in town. She'd be sorry to see Madison leave, but she was glad Madison was staying in Cedar Bay.

Roxie, who had just arrived and parked her car nearby, walked up to Kelly and said, "Woolgathering? Isn't it a little early in the morning for that?"

"Probably is, but this coffee shop and I go way back. I was reminiscing more than woolgathering. You know my grandparents started it with just a couple of tables and a tiny kitchen. I think Nana would be proud as punch that what she started so many years ago has lasted and grown. Anyway, enough of that, we better get started. Good, here come Charlie and Madison," she said, as she unlocked the door of the coffee shop.

"Understood from Mike that you and he were going to have a one day stay-at-home honeymoon, but from what I hear, it didn't even last half a day," Roxie said, hanging up her coat.

"Yeah, probably has to be one of the shortest honeymoons on record. I assume you're talking about Jesse's death," Kelly answered.

"I am, and it makes me so sad to think we were with him just the day before he was killed. Does Mike have any idea who did it?"

She started to answer when Charlie walked in. "Mornin' boss. Hear you discovered another body. Know who did it?"

"Hi, Charlie, and to answer both of your questions, the answer is no. Mike didn't get home until late last night, and I haven't had a chance to talk to him about it. And Charlie, as far as me discovering another body, I don't know what's happening in this town. I sure hope this doesn't happen again. I'm absolutely certain we're going to be just as busy as we were the day after Amber, Jeff, and Scott were murdered. People seem to need a place where they can go and talk about a tragedy and see what everyone else knows about it. Looks like Kelly's Koffee Shop is the place to go when a resident wants to find out what's happening in our sleepy little town."

"Since we're going to be busy this morning, is there something special you want me to do?" Madison asked.

"I'm going to make some bacon and cheese quiches. They're always a hit whether they're warm or cold. We'll serve them for breakfast while they're warm, and the ones that are left we can serve to the lunch crowd. Who can resist those? Plus I got in an order of oranges, so Madison, I'd like you to start squeezing oranges for the juice. Yumm, just thinking about fresh orange juice and warm cheesy bacony quiche makes my mouth water.

"I was planning on coming in yesterday afternoon, since I haven't been in here for a week because of the wedding, but with Jesse's death, it didn't work out. I need to get started on the quiches right away. Roxie, you take care of the coffee, and make sure the tables are set and ready for the customers. Charlie, I need you to set up for a busy morning. You're probably going to have a lot of omelets and short orders. I'd use the term *mise en place*, but I well remember how you told me the one time I used that phrase that you weren't French, so I should just speak plain old English. I think you told me to tell you to just get your stuff ready and forget the French words for 'put in place.' So, consider yourself told!"

At 11:00, when the breakfast crowd had thinned, Kelly walked over to Roxie and said, "Mind if I step out for about half an hour? I want to personally thank Amanda for the beautiful flower arrangements and the bouquets she did for the wedding. I'll be back in time for the lunch crowd. Okay?"

"Absolutely, Madison told me her school's on break this week, so she'll be here and we'll be fine. Take your time. Tell Amanda I agree, the flowers were absolutely beautiful."

CHAPTER SEVEN

Kelly took off her apron, walked down the pier, and crossed the street to where Amanda's Flower Shop was located. The tinkling bell that rang when she opened the door of the shop alerted Amanda that a customer had entered her shop. "Be with you in a moment. Feel free to look around," Amanda called out from the back room.

Kelly was happy to have some time to enjoy the scents and the colors of the various floral arrangements. Brightly colored roses, orchids, and gladiolas were arranged in glass vases inside the floral cooler.

Someone told me that Amanda has greenhouses on her property, and that's how she's able to have so many blooming flowers for sale. She probably uses warming lamps, because there's no way anyone could grow all these orchids this time of year in this damp climate. Not to mention the more exotic sun-loving plants like the ginger and frangipani. They're simply gorgeous. I'd like to take every one of them home with me.

"Hi, Kelly, I didn't know it was you. You know you're always welcome to come into the back room," the petite grey-haired woman in the white smock with the words "I Love Blooming Flowers" written in bright green on it said as she walked over to Kelly and gave her a friendly hug.

"Actually, I enjoyed having a few minutes to soak up the ambience of your shop. The flowers and your arrangements are simply breathtaking."

"Thanks. I've been really lucky since I opened the shop a few years ago. Flowers have always been my passion, and after Rex died it gave me something to do. I just wish I'd had the courage to do it a long time ago. People come from all around the area to buy my flowers and arrangements. I've developed quite a clientele of people who request that I do flower arrangements for their weddings, special occasions, and some customers even like me to deliver a weekly arrangement to their home or business."

"That makes me jealous. I sure wish I could afford a weekly arrangement, but the reason I'm here is I want to thank you again for the lovely flowers you provided for my wedding, the bouquets you did for Julia and me, and the floral centerpieces for the reception. Each one was spectacular, truly a work of art."

"It was my pleasure, Kelly, but would you do me a favor? If you ever get married again, don't have your wedding on Valentine's Day. That's my single busiest day of the year. I don't think I slept for several days beforehand. I fell in bed Saturday night at 7:00, and the next thing I knew it was 5:00 last night. Can you believe it? I slept for almost twenty-four hours. I got up, had a bite of dinner, went right back to bed, and didn't wake up until this morning. For the first time in several days, I feel almost normal."

When Amanda heard the little bell over the door tinkle, she turned to see who had come into the shop. "Hello, Sydney. How are you? I haven't seen you for a long time. Sydney, do you know Kelly Conner, oops, Kelly Reynolds?"

"Yes, I briefly met you a long time ago when I was in your coffee shop. It's nice to see you again."

"Thank you, and I'm sorry, but I didn't catch your last name."

"It's Allen, my name is Sydney Allen," the tall, stately looking brunette said, her gold bracelets jangling against one another. "I believe you were a good friend of my late ex-husband."

"What are you talking about?" Amanda said in a loud voice. "Your late ex-husband? What do you mean?"

"I guess you haven't heard that Jesse was murdered at The Crush yesterday. I came here today to pick something out to give to Mrs. Allen. She and Celia decided to have Jesse cremated rather than have a funeral," she said, twisting a gold bracelet around her wrist.

"Jesse's dead? What are you talking about? Kelly, have you heard about it?"

"She knows," Sydney said. "From what Jesse's sister told me, she was the one who discovered Jesse's body, she and her husband, the sheriff."

Amanda turned to Kelly. "Is that true?"

"Yes. Since you slept all day yesterday, you're probably the only one in town who hasn't heard about it."

"I can't believe it," Amanda said, sitting down heavily in a chair next to the counter. "Why would anyone want to kill Jesse? I've known him since we were in kindergarten together, and I've never heard anyone say anything bad about him."

"Well," Sydney said, turning and facing Kelly, "you might want to tell your husband he'd better start by talking to Sophie Marchant. From what I hear, it wouldn't be the first time she's done something like this."

"What do you mean? I've met her and thought she was quite lovely."

"Sure, she plays that fragile little French female role to the hilt. I heard she was interested in Jesse, so I had a private investigator see what he could find out about her. Seems her first husband was killed while she lived in France, and she was accused of murdering him. She got off because of a hung jury, and then she found some rich banker guy whose family owns the biggest perfumery in France. She convinced him to marry her and come to the United States where no one knew what had happened to her first husband. She got her just deserts, though. He left her and married some Hollywood starlet. Serves her right. Yeah, you better tell your husband to start his search for my wonderful Jesse's murderer with her. If a woman's done it once, she's certainly capable of doing it again," she said bitterly.

"That's a pretty strong accusation," Kelly said.

"Sure is, and I'm sure it's well-deserved. Jesse and I were talking about reconciling, probably even remarrying, until he met her. Mark my words, that woman either knows something about his death or she did it."

"Sydney," Kelly said, "I can certainly understand why you're upset, but what motive could she possibly have for wanting him dead? If they were seeing one another, it doesn't make any sense for her to want to kill him."

"Talk is she's been seeing a married man during the week when she's staying at her other home up in Portland. Who knows? Jesse may have found out about it and gotten angry. Maybe they had words. She's involved, somehow. I know it in my bones."

Kelly looked at her watch. "Amanda, Sydney, I have to leave and get back to the coffee shop. I've been gone long enough. Amanda, once again, thank you for everything. Sydney, I'm very sorry about Jesse, but I have to tell you, I'm having a hard time seeing Sophie as his murderer." She opened the door and the little bell above the door tinkled as she left the shop.

I wonder if Celia and Sydney spend every moment of the day talking about how horrible Sophie is. They must feed off of each other. I've learned over the years to trust my instincts and my instincts aren't usually wrong. I sure hope they're not this time, because I really did like Sophie and her grief seemed genuine.

CHAPTER EIGHT

As Kelly crossed the street on her way back to the coffee shop, she saw Mike's black and white patrol car pulling into the parking lot next to the pier with Rebel riding shotgun. She ran over and hugged Mike as he got out of the car followed by Rebel. "Hello, Sheriff Mike, how's my husband today?" she asked, grinning.

"A lot better after a nice hug like that, but I could use some coffee and lunch. I've been looking at files and on the phone all morning," he said as the three of them walked into Kelly's. It was busy, but Kelly's trained eye spotted an open table, and she told him to hurry and sit down before someone else took the spot.

"I need to talk to Roxie a minute, and then I'll get your coffee. Take a look at the board, but I'd recommend the baked burritos with chicken and beans. I happen to know that's one of your favorites."

"Don't need to look. That's what I want, and yes, it definitely is one of my favorites. Take your time," he said, quickly reaching into his pocket for a treat for Rebel as Kelly walked away with her back to them.

She returned a few minutes later with his coffee. "Mike, I went over to Amanda's Flower Shop a little while ago. I wanted to thank her in person for the flowers she did for the wedding, but I need to talk to you about some things I found out while I was there. Give me a couple more minutes, and then I can sit down. Madison's on break from classes this week, so she and Roxie can handle the start of the lunchtime crowd."

"No problem. I could use a break myself."

Five minutes later she returned with his burritos and a fresh cup of coffee. "Mike, I don't know what you've found out, but I've had a couple of interesting conversations that I need to share with you." She told him about her talks with Mrs. Allen and Celia, with Sophie, and finally her encounter with Sydney while she was at the flower shop.

When she was finished talking, Mike put his coffee cup down and wiped his mouth with his napkin. "Kelly," he said in a voice that sounded extremely aggravated, "I know you well enough by now to know if I asked you to stop talking to possible suspects in one of my cases that you wouldn't. I also know you well enough to know you'd probably have an excuse for going to see Mrs. Allen and Sophie..."

She interrupted him, "Mike, please don't be upset with me. As a matter of fact, I told you I was going to Mrs. Allen's home. I didn't want her to find out about her son's death from someone else, and it was a plausible reason, not an excuse. As for Sophie Marchant, I hadn't planned on going there at all, but once I found out that she and Jesse were very close, it seemed like the right thing to do, rather than have her find out from some television report or read it in the headline of the local newspaper. You can call those excuses if you want, but I certainly don't," she said. "As for meeting Jesse's ex-wife, Sydney Allen, at Amanda's Flower Shop, how could that possibly be an excuse? It was purely a random thing. How was I to know she'd walk in the flower shop while I was there?"

"I have no idea, but you probably saw her walking down the street or something," he said raising his eyebrows and taking another sip of coffee. "Oh well, I know I'm not going to get anywhere with this. What do you make of these women? Sounds like a lot of female cat-fighting to me."

"I honestly don't know. It's pretty obvious that Sydney and Celia hate Sophie. I liked her, but if what Sydney says is true, then she certainly didn't tell me everything about her background."

"To play the devil's advocate, why should she? You were someone who had just told her the man she loved had been murdered. There was no reason for her to tell you about her first husband's death and the trial, if it's true."

"No, you're right. I only asked her about how she happened to come to the United States," she said as she paused and looked around the room. "I can't stay much longer. Looks like we're getting busy, and I've got to help Roxie and Madison. Anyway, what did you find out?"

"Something I sure wasn't expecting. I found out The Crush has been losing money for months, and that Jesse owed back taxes and was way behind on the payments he was supposed to make to the wineries that supplied him with the wine he sold. He was big time, seriously, in debt. I've been going through his files all morning, and I found something else that I thought was very interesting."

"What?"

"Many years ago when he was still married to Sydney, he'd taken an insurance policy out on his life in the amount of one million dollars. Evidently he never changed the beneficiary after his divorce, because Sydney is still named as the primary beneficiary."

"Wow! That would sure give her a motive to kill him. Jesse dies and bingo, she gets a million bucks."

"That's what I thought, too, but if she wanted to reconcile with him, and she even hoped they might remarry, it doesn't make a lot of sense for her to kill him. I wonder if she even knew he'd never changed the beneficiary on the policy after they got divorced."

"Sorry, Mike, but I've got to stop our conversation. I need to help Roxie and Madison. Before I go, let me tell you something. At our reception I noticed Jesse was perspiring heavily and although it was a beautiful day, it was still cool. He didn't look like his normal self. From what you've just told me that might be the reason. Perhaps he was worrying about his debts, or maybe one of his creditors was even threatening him.

"I really do have to go. This place is completely full, and I can see people standing outside, waiting to be seated, but I just had a thought. Remember when Luke told me Jesse was going to give him a crash course in winemaking when he decided to take over the White Cloud Retreat Center? I wonder if Luke knows anything about Jesse? Would it be okay with you if I give him a call this afternoon?"

"Sweetheart," he said in an exasperated voice, "would it even matter if I asked you not to? Or would it even matter if I told you that it was my case, and I should be the one who called Luke? Or would it matter if I told you I really don't want you involved in this case, because it deals with murder and I worry about you?"

"Of course it would matter," she said, mentally crossing her fingers behind her back.

"Somehow I doubt that, but since you know Luke better than I do, you probably should be the one to talk to him. I know you've become friends. Maybe you can find something out from him."

"Thanks for the vote of confidence. I've got to get back to work. I'll call him later on and tell you tonight what he had to say. You will be home for dinner tonight, won't you?"

"Yes, there's not much work I can do tonight on the case. I'm trying to find out from the IRS how much Jesse owed in back taxes, and there are a bunch of other past due bills in some of his files I need to look at. I haven't run across the name of a tax person or anything like that yet. I'd like to ask his ex-wife if she knows if he had one, but since I've found out she's the beneficiary of his life insurance policy and a possible suspect, I'm a little reluctant to do that."

"I could ask his mother."

"Don't push it, Kelly. I've been more than generous by agreeing to let you call Luke. My generosity ends there. Fair enough?"

"Fair enough, and I love you."

"Love you too, Mrs. Reynolds," he said standing up, taking his signature white Stetson hat from the hat rack near the door, and walking out of the coffee shop with Rebel closely following. As soon as the door closed behind them, Mike reached into his pocket for Rebel's customary treat. "Our little secret, boy. Don't think she'd approve," he said, as they walked to his sheriff's car.

CHAPTER NINE

"Kelly, phone's for you," Roxie said, handing it to Kelly.

"This is Kelly, may I help you?"

"Hi, Kelly, or I suppose it would be more appropriate for me to say 'Hi Mrs. Reynolds, given the fact of your recent name change. This is Doc, and I wanted to tell you your wedding was beautiful. I was honored that you and Mike would have me be a part of it. Guess Mike will be standing up for me in the not too distant future when Liz and I tie the knot. Your wedding gave Liz and me a lot of food for thought, but I sure hope we don't have all the uninvited guests you had."

"It's we who thank you, Doc, for standing up with Mike, and I agree, it was a beautiful wedding, although I feel so badly about what happened to Jesse."

"Me, too. I really liked him. Whenever I went to The Crush to get a bottle of wine, he was always so patient with me, explaining all about the different wines. He's really going to be missed."

"Speaking of which, you're not at the coffee shop, and it's noon. Something must be pretty important for you to miss eating lunch here. Is everything okay?"

"Yes, everything's fine. Somehow our scheduler here at the clinic overbooked me with patients, but I would like to talk to you. I was hoping to do it at lunch, but that's simply not going to be possible today. There's no way I can get out of here. I think half the people in Cedar Bay have the flu. Any chance you could stop by the clinic this afternoon?"

"Sure. Can you schedule a little time for me around 3:00 or so?"

"I'll tell the receptionist to notify me as soon as you come in. I'll make it work."

"Want to tell me what this is about?"

"No, I just heard something I thought might be of interest to you. Don't have enough to tell Mike about it, so I thought I'd get your input."

"Sounds interesting. See you at 3:00. Want me to bring you a doggie bag when I come?"

"A little something for me, and a little something for Lucky would be very much appreciated. Thank you!"

She walked into the kitchen where Madison was refilling her coffee pot. It was a chilly day, and Kelly had lost count of how many pots of coffee they'd made in the large commercial coffee urn.

"Madison, Charlie, I'm making a little care package for Doc. He's overloaded with patients and can't make it in for lunch today. I'm going to take him two of the chicken burritos we've been serving. I'm writing 'Hands Off' on it, so neither one of you will accidentally serve it to a customer."

"Got it, boss. I'll keep an eye on it for you," Charlie said.

"Thanks."

She took her cell phone out of her purse intending to call Luke and went into the storeroom for a little privacy.

"Hi, Luke, it's Kelly."

"You must have ESP. I was getting ready to call you and offer my congratulations to both you and Sheriff Mike. That was a beautiful ceremony. I just wish Scott could have been here to see it."

"So do I, and I also wish Amber could have been at the wedding. I'm not sure you ever met her, but she was my godchild."

"No, I didn't, but I remember reading about her tragic death in the newspaper. As I recall, she was an only child. How are her parents doing?"

"It's been terribly hard on them. As a matter of fact, I was thinking of visiting them this afternoon. Doc asked me to stop by the clinic and see him, and the book store Ginger owns is only a block down the street from him. I want to thank her in person for taking care of the wedding guest book at the church."

"I wondered who that was. I've met a lot of people in Cedar Bay since I came to the Center, but I've not met her."

"I'm not surprised. It's taken her awhile to recover from Amber's murder. I think the wedding was really her first venture out in public other than going to work at her book store. She and her husband have pretty much been holed up in their house. I've gone over to see them a few times and frankly, they're not doing very well. They both seem to be hopelessly overcome with grief and sadness from the loss of their daughter. Jim's handyman business has become almost non-existent, and you know what's happened to private book stores since people can buy a book on the Internet a lot cheaper than they can buy the same book at a book store."

"I didn't know there was a handyman in town. I've got several things that I need to get fixed out here. Would you mind giving me his name and telephone number?"

"Here it is," Kelly said. "I know he'll be happy to get some work. I've used him for years and highly recommend him."

"Good to know. Thanks. So what can I do for you?"

"I remember after Scott's death you told me that Jesse was going to give you a crash course in winemaking. I'm wondering how that turned out."

"You've got a good memory. We met a number of times since last November, and his help and advice was invaluable to me. I'm really sorry to hear of his death. Interesting you'd ask me about wine making, because this morning the Pellino brothers paid me a visit. You know, they're the ones who own the vineyard next to ours. They're the same guys Scott had a run-in with before he was killed over their improper use of dangerous chemicals banned by the EPA."

"So you're telling me they came to see you? That's a first, isn't it?"

"That's true, but I don't quite know what to make of it."

"I'm very interested in hearing what they had to say."

"It was an awkward conversation. They wanted to know if I was planning on selling the Center now that Jesse was dead. I asked them why Jesse's death would cause me to sell the Center, and then I told them I had absolutely no plans to sell it. They said they wanted to buy it, and now with Jesse dead they figured I wouldn't know how to make good wine, and I might as well sell the vineyard to them. They told me they'd give me a fair price, and they could pay the entire purchase price in cash, since they didn't need to get a bank loan."

"You're kidding!" Kelly interrupted. "I remember Jesse saying there was some talk that their money might be Mafia money. What do you think?"

"I have no idea. I'm not planning on selling the property, but if I was, it wouldn't be cheap and for someone to pay all cash for it? I suppose it could be Mafia money. I don't know many people who have that much available cash."

"I know I may be jumping the gun here, but it almost seems to me like they might have a motive for killing Jesse. If Jesse was dead and couldn't help you with the winemaking, you might be inclined to sell the property to them. Maybe their intent is to try and convince you that you don't have the necessary skills to make the fine wine that Scott was able to make. Does that sound crazy?"

"No, not at all. I think you're right, and I've just made a decision. I've been debating with myself for the last month whether I may be in over my head with the winemaking part of the Center. There are so many other things to do here that I just can't devote myself to it exclusively. I met a great guy at the Oregon Wine Conference Scott and I attended several months ago before he was killed. He's a wine and vineyard consultant. I think I'll hire him to come here and help me. The Center has the money, and with Jesse gone, I really do need some help. I don't want to be the one responsible for having to sell the Center because of lost revenue from lower wine sales, and I sure don't want it to go into the hands of the Pellino brothers."

"I think that's a great idea. How long are you planning on hiring this consultant to work at the Center?"

"I don't know. If he's able to come here for several months, that would be great. I can easily put him up here. I'll let you know. Kelly, I just thought of something else. I overheard the Pellino brothers talking when they left, and I'm pretty sure they didn't mean for me to hear what they said. It was kind of a veiled threat."

"What did they say?"

"Well, like I said, it wasn't said directly to me, but I overheard Dante tell Luca that, and I quote, 'He might want to take a lesson from what happened to Jesse.' The meeting I had with them took place here in my office. There's a gap in my office window frame, so I can often hear what people say when they walk past it on their way to the parking lot. That's how I overheard what Dante said. Since he didn't say it directly to me, I suppose technically it's not a threat. By the way, that's one of the reasons I'm glad I got the name of Bob, the handyman, from you. I need to have some caulking put in around the window in my office."

"The threat may not have been said directly to you, Luke, but I sure would consider it a threat. Be careful. I remember you had a .22 pistol that you started keeping in your desk and nightstand after Scott was murdered. If you've put it somewhere else, you might want to rescue it and get in the habit of keeping it handy."

"Good advice. Thanks for the call. I need to see about getting in touch with the wine consultant and also Bob, the handyman you recommended. Talk to you later."

If the Pellino brothers are tied to the Mafia, I sure wouldn't want to get on the wrong side of them, and it sounds like Luke is. I wonder how far they'd go to get control of the Center's property.

CHAPTER TEN

Kelly heated up the burritos in the microwave and cut up some chicken for Lucky. When the burritos were ready she locked the coffee shop door, and she and Lady walked out to her minivan. Lady's nose kept drifting in the direction of the cloth bag holding the food Kelly had prepared for Doc.

"Not now, girl. When we get to the clinic, you and Lucky can each have a treat, but not before."

Five minutes later they walked through the front door of the Cedar Bay Clinic, an attractive brick building with yellow shutters on each side of the windows and a yellow canopy over the door. It was an inviting, warm building, a place that welcomed the visitors, whether they were seeing Liz, the town's psychologist, or Doc, the town's medical doctor. No matter what they needed help with, they began their visit in a friendly and inviting atmosphere.

"Would you please tell Doc that Kelly Reynolds is here to see him? Thanks," she said to the young receptionist, as she looked around approvingly at the room which had vases filled with cut flowers and vivid green plants on the tables. Photographs and paintings of Cedar Bay filled the walls.

The young woman called Doc on the intercom, then turned to Kelly and said, "He asked me to take you back to his office. Please follow me."

Kelly and Lady walked into Doc's large office where he was sitting behind his desk. Lucky, the yellow Labrador retriever Kelly had given to him as a present, was in his dog bed next to Doc. One wall was covered with the framed diplomas and honors Doc had obtained over the years. Two of the walls had early 20th century California Impressionist paintings on them, and bookcases filled with books covered the fourth wall.

"Doc, it looks like you've put some of the paintings you inherited from your family on the walls here in your office. This is the first time I've been in your office, and I want to tell you I think it looks great. I love the warm pale yellow paint. It's very soothing and comforting."

"I read somewhere that if patients feel at ease in a doctor's office, they heal a lot faster. There's nothing worse for a patient than to sit in some sterile doctor's office with austere white walls and nothing to welcome them. They're already nervous about having a problem serious enough to require a visit to the doctor's office, so no sense making it worse for them."

"I'm sure you're right. I bet your patients love your office, well as much as anyone's going to love going to a doctor's office. Here's the care package I promised you – two chicken and bean burritos with some of my own favorite bacon chocolate chip cookies from the secret stash I keep in the freezer. I also brought a treat for Lucky, and I have enough for Lady as well. Don't think she'd be very happy about Lucky getting a treat if she didn't." She handed him the casserole dish with the burritos and divided up the rest of the chicken for the two dogs.

"This looks delicious, Kelly, thank you so much, and Lucky thanks you too."

"My pleasure. Can't let my best customer starve! You don't seem like your usual self today, Doc. What's wrong?"

"Sorry, I didn't realize it was that apparent. Even though I said I wasn't going to call Mike about it, something's telling me I probably should. Since you're here, I'll tell you if you promise you won't do anything with the information other than tell Mike."

"I promise," she said, mentally crossing her fingers behind her back just in case.

"Jesse Allen's mother was in here this morning. Poor thing is taking the loss of her son pretty hard. There's no reason to tell you why she came to see me, that's confidential and not important to what I'm going to tell you, but what isn't confidential is what she told me. She said she hadn't been fully honest with Mike when he called her this morning. She asked me if I would give him a message for her. I said I'd be happy to, as you and Mike were good friends of mine. I told her I'd been best man at his recent wedding where Jesse had provided the wine."

"What did she tell you, and what did she tell Mike?" Kelly asked.

"It isn't so much what she told Mike, it's more about what she didn't tell him."

"Like what?"

"Last night she was looking for anything that would help her sleep and she remembered that Celia had some sleeping pills she'd gotten from me some time ago because of her chronic problems with insomnia. Celia wasn't home at the time, so she couldn't ask her where they were. She looked in the medicine cabinet in Celia's bathroom and couldn't find them, but then she remembered Celia saying something about keeping them handy next to her bed. She told me she opened the drawer of Celia's nightstand and didn't see them. She was sure Celia had told her they were in the drawer, so she took it completely out of the nightstand. At the very back of the drawer were the pills."

"That doesn't sound so unusual."

"No, it wasn't. What was unusual was the gun that was taped to the underneath side of the drawer. She told me the only way anyone could see the gun was if the drawer was completely removed from the nightstand."

"What does Mrs. Allen think?"

"She doesn't know what to think. When Mike called her this morning and asked her if she'd noticed anything unusual about Jesse or anything else, she'd told him no. She told me she felt guilty for not telling him about the gun she'd discovered, and asked if I would tell Mike about it. She said she was too emotionally distraught to call him."

"Did she give you any indication why Celia would have a gun taped to the underneath side of her nightstand drawer?"

"No. She said she couldn't imagine why Celia had the gun. The only thing she could think of was that Celia had been married to a policeman who died quite a few years ago. That's when she moved in with her mother. Mrs. Allen wonders if the gun was his, and Celia keeps it there as a remembrance of him."

"I think that's very strange, Doc, but I wonder if this gun might provide some link to Jesse's death. Did she say what kind of a gun it was?"

"She said she doesn't know anything about guns, but she pulled back the tape on the gun, and saw where it was stamped with '.38 S&W.' I know quite a bit about guns, and it sounds to me like it's a .38 caliber Smith & Wesson, but I couldn't say for sure without seeing it. As far as a link to Jesse's death, I don't see one. It just strikes me as very odd that a woman would have a gun taped to the bottom of her nightstand drawer. I have to say it made me wonder what caliber of gun killed Jesse. You can see why I wasn't comfortable calling Mike with it. I just didn't feel it was important enough to call him, but something bothers me about it. Celia was the one who brought her mother to the clinic today, and she seems like a very unsettled and angry woman. I've treated her before, and while I've always had that impression, today it was even more so."

"She may be angry and yes, angry people often kill, but her own brother? I just can't connect the dots in that scenario."

"Nor can I, but as I said, Mrs. Allen asked me to tell Mike, and I promised her I would. Would you tell him for me?"

"Doc, of course I will. How can you even think I wouldn't?" Kelly asked in a hurt voice.

"Just trying to keep you from doing anything Mike wouldn't be happy about. As I recall, it's happened before. You can plan on it that I'll mention it to Mike the next time I see him. Sure would hate for him to hear it from me for the first time a couple of days or weeks from now," he said with a twinkle in his eye, his meaning clear.

"You have my word, Doc. I'll tell him tonight. Speaking of which, I better leave. I need to stop by Ginger's book shop on the way home, and I don't want to be late. If there aren't signs of dinner being prepared, Mike may wonder if he made a mistake last Saturday when he married me. Time for us to go. Lady, come," she said, standing up and walking over to the door. "You can bring that dish back to the coffee shop when you come for lunch tomorrow. Believe me, there are plenty more where that came from."

"Lucky and I are grateful for the care packages, aren't we Lucky?"

Lucky voiced his approval with a resounding bark.

A gun taped to the underneath side of Celia's nightstand. That's really strange. Wonder how Jesse and Celia got along. I know Celia's close with Jesse's ex-wife, Sydney, but like I told Doc, I can't connect any dots. Maybe Mike can come up with something.

CHAPTER ELEVEN

After leaving the clinic, Kelly drove her minivan the short distance to Ginger's book store, appropriately named The Book Nook. It was located in a quaint little early 20th century brick building with two large bay windows on either side of the front door. Inside the store Ginger had installed cozy window seats next to the bay windows with comfortable red and white checkered cushions. Customers often took several books from the shelves and sat in the window seats while they leafed through the books, deciding which ones to buy. The smell of potpourri and freshly made ginger tea also gave the little shop a warm, inviting ambience along with a fire which was always burning in the fireplace.

It would really be a shame if Ginger had to close this little shop. It's one of the most charming shops in Cedar Bay, plus it's been Ginger's salvation since Amber died. I'm not sure she could have survived the overwhelming grief and despair she felt after Amber's murder if she hadn't had the Book Nook.

"Kelly, Lady, how wonderful to see you. I understand your blushing bride role didn't last too long," Ginger said, giving Kelly a hug and reaching into a jar she kept handy to get a treat for Lady. The Book Nook welcomed dogs, and Ginger kept a large bowl of water just outside the front door for the ones that were thirsty as well as the jar of treats she kept next to the cash register.

"I want to thank you again for overseeing the guest book at the wedding. It was a huge help, and as I told you when I asked you to do it, you certainly would have been my maid of honor if Julia couldn't do it."

"No problem. I'm glad she was able to be your maid of honor. With Cash giving you away and Julia there, it was perfect for the circumstances. It really was a lovely wedding, but I was so sorry to hear about Jesse. He loved to read and came in here a lot over the years. I used to call him whenever I got any new books in about wine. I think he singlehandedly bought every book I ever stocked on the subject. We're all going to miss him. I'm glad you stopped by because I heard something today that Mike should probably be aware of. Why don't you have a seat over by the window, and I'll get us some tea."

A few minutes later when they were seated and had their tea, Kelly asked, "What did you hear and from whom?"

"You know there are a couple of Alcoholics Anonymous groups that hold their meetings at different locations here in town. A few months ago I was asked by one of the members if I would mind opening up the Book Nook on Monday mornings so a meeting could be held here. Evidently they couldn't meet any longer at one of the other places they'd been using. I told them I'd be happy to do it. Actually, between you and me, I'd do about anything to bring more people into the store. Anyway, they started meeting here about three months ago. I open up an hour before my regular opening time and spend their meeting time restocking the shelves and doing bookkeeping. They bring the chairs in from around the store and make a circle. There aren't very many people in the group, perhaps no more than six or eight."

"I don't see how this might be something that would be of interest to Mike."

"I'm getting to that. On several occasions I've overheard one particular man say really bad things about The Crush."

"You're kidding. What did he say?"

"I heard him say it was stores like The Crush that caused people to become alcoholics. I've also heard him say that all liquor stores should be put out of business, and their owners should be run out of town. A couple of times I even heard him say that the liquor store owners were doing the devil's work, and God or someone else should take them out, so the stores would permanently close. I really didn't pay much attention to it. I considered it kind of idle rambling from someone who must be having a difficult time giving up alcohol, however this morning it was different. He was here as usual, but instead of feeling bad about Jesse's death, I overheard him say he was really happy Jesse had been killed, and how he hoped The Crush would close permanently. I think his exact words were 'Aren't you all glad that someone had the courage to kill Jesse Allen? That's one less man to do the devil's work.' It kind of frightened me."

"It frightens me as well. Do you have any idea who this man is?"

"None, and since one of the cornerstones of the Alcoholics Anonymous organization is anonymity, I don't think anyone would tell me, even if they knew."

"Unfortunately, you're probably right. I'll tell Mike about it, but I'm not sure how he could find out either. Thanks, Ginger. By the way, I was talking to Luke Monroe earlier today, and he said he was going to talk to Bob about doing some handyman repairs out at the Center."

"Thank you. Bob called me earlier and told me Luke had called him. He's meeting with Luke tomorrow. I didn't know it was because of you that Luke called Bob, but we really appreciate it, and Bob can sure use the work. We're going through some tough times, and I don't know how much longer we can hold on financially."

"Glad I could help. You're good people," Kelly said as she stood up and gave Ginger a hug. "Time for me to get home and see what I can come up with for dinner tonight. Sometimes I think that might be the only reason why Mike married me. I can almost guarantee you that if I wasn't a good cook, I wouldn't be Mrs. Reynolds."

"Somehow I doubt that."

"I don't," Kelly said walking out. "See you soon! Lady, come."

CHAPTER TWELVE

Kelly pulled into the driveway just as Mike and Rebel were getting out of his patrol car. Mike walked over to her van and opened the door for Kelly and Lady, kissing her on the cheek and giving Lady a pat on the head.

"We've got to stop meeting this way," he said, grinning. "Kind of nice to come home to my wife. You're the best thing that's happened to me all day!"

"Keep talking like that and you might qualify for one of my famous dinners. Actually I think we'll have Reuben sandwiches tonight. It's been a stressful couple of days for both of us. A glass of wine, a fire, a Reuben sandwich, and then a piece of that raspberry tart from the wedding reception. Doesn't that sound divine?"

"I thought everything got eaten at the reception," Mike said. "Have you been holding out on me?"

"Well, I know how much you love that tart, so before the first guest even arrived, I asked Roxie if she'd put two pieces in the refrigerator in the garage."

"Smart thinking, but then again, I've never heard anyone accuse you of being stupid, but I have to admit, that may be in the realm of downright brilliant thinking."

"Thank you, Sheriff Mike. Go change clothes and I'll open the wine."

"Will do. I'll be back shortly."

A few minutes later Kelly handed him a glass of wine and said, "I've had quite an afternoon. I've got a lot to tell you, but you probably do too. You want to go first?"

"No. I spent the afternoon looking through Jesse's files. Not much to tell there. Anyway, my mother raised me to be a gentleman, and ladies are always supposed to go first. You're up."

She started by relating her conversation with Luke about the Pellino brothers and their interest in buying the White Cloud Retreat Center. Mike interrupted her, "Was a dollar amount mentioned? That's some pretty valuable acreage, and I don't see the Pellino brothers having that kind of money. They sell the bulk of the wines they produce to discount chains. A Mafia connection would make a lot of sense, and there have been rumors that they just might be Family."

"If there was a dollar amount, Luke didn't mention it to me, but that's not all Luke told me. I haven't even told you about the veiled threat." She explained what Luke had heard Dante say to Luca when they were outside the Center and walked past Luke's slightly broken window.

"I definitely would consider that a threat if I was Luke. I'd also think with all the people around the Center, it's probably a pretty safe place, but that hasn't always been true in the past. Dante and Luca both have very distinctive looking appearances. If they were anywhere near The Crush around the time of the murder, someone would remember them. It probably wouldn't hurt for me to put something in the newspaper and on TV asking people to call my office if they saw or heard any unusual activity around The Crush in the hours before the murder. I'll do it tomorrow."

"I think that's an excellent idea, but I have a couple of other things to tell you and…"

"What do you mean you have a couple of other things to tell me?" Mike said, raising his eyebrows. "I told you it was all right for you to call Luke. I never suggested that you do anything else concerning my investigation."

"Doc called and wanted to talk to me. He didn't think what he had to tell me was important enough to bother you with, then he changed his mind, but I told him I'd tell you and save him the trouble. Evidently Mrs. Allen didn't tell you everything when you questioned her."

"What are you talking about? I had a long conversation with her this morning."

"You may have, but she felt guilty that she hadn't told you about the gun she found in Celia's nightstand. It was a .38 Smith & Wesson, and it was taped to the underneath side of her nightstand drawer."

"What! A gun in the nightstand! No, she definitely did not tell me about it."

"That's what she told Doc. Celia took her in today to see Doc, and Mrs. Allen felt bad she hadn't told you about finding the gun. She told Doc about it and asked him if he would tell you."

"Okay, Kelly, tell me the whole story."

When she was finished, he went over to the counter and poured himself another glass of wine. "Want a refill?"

"No thanks. Mike, why can't you just go to the Allen home, get the gun, and have a ballistics test run on it to see if it matches the bullet that killed Jesse?"

"Wish I could, sweetheart, but I'd need a search warrant, and I don't have enough facts to present to the court to get a search warrant issued. I mean, she had a gun in her bedroom. So what? A lot of people have guns in their bedrooms. No, there's no way a court would grant a search warrant without a greater showing of probable cause, and there's not enough here for probable cause."

"Too bad. I need to start dinner in a few minutes, but there's one more thing I need to tell you."

"How do these things always seem to happen to you, when I'm the county sheriff, and this is my case? Never mind, even if you knew you probably wouldn't tell me. I'm beginning to think you're one of those people who just walks easy on the earth. Is what you're about to tell me the last thing you found out today? Had a rather busy day, didn't you, love?"

"Mike, stop it. I can't help it, honest, these things just somehow seem to happen to me."

When she finished telling him about what Ginger had overheard during the Alcoholics Anonymous meeting, he sat back in his chair, turning the wine glass in his hands, deep in thought.

"So from what you heard today, there could possibly be three suspects, is that right?" he asked.

"You're the sheriff, I'm not, but yes, I think Celia would qualify as a suspect since she had a gun hidden in her nightstand. Other than being brother and sister, I have no idea what the relationship was between Jesse and Celia, or what possible motive she might have for wanting to kill Jesse, but maybe I should talk to her."

"No Kelly, if anyone is going to talk to her, I should be the one to do it."

"Right, you're absolutely right, Sheriff Mike. That was simply a slip of the tongue on my part."

"Uh-huh."

"Anyway, back to the suspects," she said. "So we have, sorry, I meant to say you have Celia, the Pellino brothers, and I'm kind of wondering about the guy at the Book Nook. He might qualify as a suspect."

"True, but the problem is the members of the group are anonymous and we don't know who he is. I don't think they even use their last names. I doubt if there's a sign-in sheet or anything with their names on it. Kelly, I can see something going on in your mind. What are you thinking?"

"Just wondering what I should serve with the Reubens, Mike, nothing all that important," she said innocently, glad he didn't have access to her mind. *I think I know how I can find out the identity of the man at the Book Nook.*

Later, as they were finishing dinner, Mike said, "I don't know how you can make a simple sandwich taste so good, but that was a perfect way to end the day. Now for that raspberry tart."

"I'll be back in a minute. I never brought the pieces in from the refrigerator in the garage," she said, carrying their dinner plates over to the sink. When she walked back into the room with the two tart pieces she saw Mike talking on his cell phone. She set a piece of the tart in front of him. He mouthed the words "Thank you," and continued to listen as someone talked.

"Thanks Leo, at least that gives us something solid to go on. I appreciate your calling after hours. Enjoy your evening."

"Who was that, the coroner?"

"Yes. This is starting to get interesting," Mike said, putting a piece of the tart on his fork. "This has to be the prettiest and best non-chocolate dish ever." He continued, "Leo said he was pretty sure that the bullet he took from Jesse's body was fired from a .38 caliber pistol. He's sending it to the state police and they'll give it to their ballistics expert for confirmation. Considering how long Leo's been at this, I think I can take it to the bank that Jesse was killed by a .38 caliber pistol."

"If he's right, that's the same caliber gun that was in Celia's nightstand."

"Believe me, sweetheart, I'm well aware of that, but the question remains, is that the gun that killed Jesse? Even if it is, it doesn't necessarily mean that Celia did it. I know it's quite a coincidence, but it still wouldn't hold up in a court of law or before a jury. They want facts, and the fact they would demand to know is who used that gun to kill Jesse."

"I see what you mean. Don't forget about Sydney, his ex-wife. If she knows about the life insurance policy, that's a pretty good motive, and she and Celia are good friends. She might have even known that Celia had hidden the gun in her nightstand. She could have removed the gun from under the nightstand drawer, shot poor Jesse with it and then returned the gun back to its hiding place in the nightstand. Once Jesse is dead, she gets the life insurance money."

"Well, I see that I have my work cut out for me for the next couple of days. Should be interesting."

That it should be, Kelly thought. *Now I need to see if I can find out some more about the Book Nook guy. I have a feeling about him.*

CHAPTER THIRTEEN

Kelly had just finished putting the dishes in the dishwasher and was getting ready to join Mike and watch one of their favorite television shows when her cell phone rang.

She looked at the monitor, and saw that it was Julia. "Hi, darling. Appreciated the message from you last night that you and Cash made it back safely, and that you were able to get him to the airport in plenty of time to catch his flight. Actually, I was going to call you later on and thank you for coming up here and for all your help with the wedding. I do have some bad news. Remember Jesse Allen, the man who provided all the wine for the reception? The sad thing is he was shot and killed yesterday in his shop. Mike and I were the ones who discovered him. Mike has no idea who did it, so that's kind of overshadowed our post-wedding plans. We only had a honeymoon for about half a day."

"Oh, Mom, I'm so sorry. He seemed like such a nice man. Was he married or did he have any children?"

"No, he's divorced, and to my knowledge he never had any children. I know his mother and sister. They both live here in Cedar Bay. His father passed away about a year ago. He was one of the regulars at the coffee shop, and towards the end I used to take his favorite foods to him at home a couple of times a week. I feel sorry for his mother. She's a nice woman, and she said something to me when I told her about Jesse that's so sad. She said no mother was supposed to outlive her children. You just never think you'll outlive your children."

"Please give her my condolences if you see her. I assume you'll be going to the funeral."

"I don't think so. I heard today she'd decided not to have one. She's going to have him cremated. Evidently she felt she couldn't go through another funeral. Her daughter, Celia, moved in with her after her divorce, so at least she's not alone. I think she and Jesse were pretty close. My heart really goes out to her, but enough of that. How are things in San Francisco?"

"Things are good. I wanted to talk to you a little more about Brad and his daughters. I have a huge favor to ask of Mike. Do you think there's any chance he could have a DNA test run on Brad and his daughters? I was able to get strands of hair from all three of them without any of them finding out, and I was hoping Mike could use them for a DNA test. I really don't want Brad to know about this in case it turns out badly."

"Mike and I talked briefly about it. He's concerned about what would happen if it turns out that Brad's not the father of the girls."

"He'll never know. I've decided not to tell him anything about this. If it's good news, of course I'll share it with him, and he'll be ecstatic, but if it's bad news, I'll keep it to myself."

"Julia, that's a big secret to keep all to yourself, and starting a marriage off with a big secret like that could present some problems down the road. Marriage is all wine and roses in the beginning, but as time goes by there will be some bumps in the road. I don't know of any marriage that's been one hundred percent wine and roses, and if someone says theirs is, it's been my experience they're not being honest, or their head is stuck in the sand."

"I know what you're saying, Mom, and I understand why you're saying it, but if Mike can't or won't do it, I'll find someone in San

Francisco to do it. I see ads for that kind of thing all the time. I even saw one recently where if you sent a sample of your dog's hair in to them, their lab could tell you what kind of breed the dog was. I do have to admit it sounded kind of far-fetched, but maybe it's legit. Anyway, do you think Mike would do it for me?"

"I don't know. I'll talk to him a little more about it."

"Actually, Mom, I sent the hair samples off to you by FedEx this afternoon. You should have it tomorrow morning. How long do you think it will take?"

"I have no idea. I know Mike is pretty reluctant about getting involved in this. I've heard that there can be a long wait to get the results, but if Mike's willing, he might be able to have it done on a priority basis. Let me see what he says, and I'll call you tomorrow."

"Mom, I really appreciate it, and don't worry. I have a feeling everything's going to work out fine."

"All right, if you say so, and you're the one who knows Brad. I don't. I'm just telling you what I think, but the ultimate decision is yours, and it sounds like you've made up your mind."

"I've got to go. I have to help Brad give the girls their nightly bath. Talk to you tomorrow or the day after."

"Bye, love."

Mike looked at her when she walked into the room where he was watching television. "Everything okay?" he asked.

"Yes and no. I just hope Julia knows what she's doing. We'll be getting test samples of Brad's and the girls' hair tomorrow by FedEx."

"So she decided to go ahead with the DNA test, right?"

"Yes. You probably heard my end of the conversation. I'm not sure it's a good idea."

"Well Mom, I've never had children, but I've often heard that at some point in time a child has to cut the apron strings. Seems like she's snipped yours. I know this probably isn't going to make either one of you happy, but after thinking about it, I just don't want to get involved. It could be a disaster for all of us. I'll call Julia in a day or so and tell her why I've made that decision, so you don't have to get involved."

"I can't say I'm happy about your decision, but I understand why. No matter what you tell her I'm still going to be in the middle of it. I'll just have to make the most of it. I wish she'd never asked. You know, when I was a young girl, I remember thinking when I grew up I'd be able to control everything in my life once I was an adult. I thought I would be able to do whatever I wanted to do. I've certainly found that not to be true. Here I am with a friend murdered, and I don't know who did it, and my daughter is sending her fiancé's DNA evidence to us in hopes a lab will confirm that he's the father of the girls he calls his daughters. No, I'm definitely not in control. Seems like the outside forces are winning!"

"Why don't you stick to just worrying about Julia and let me worry about the murder?"

"Okay. It probably would make my life easier."

"Wrong, sweetheart, I think you have it backwards. I think it would make my life easier!"

CHAPTER FOURTEEN

"Mornin' Madison. How are you?" Kelly asked as she walked up to the door of the coffee shop.

"I'm enjoying this week with no classes. It's nice to have a little time when I don't have to study every spare minute of the day."

"I'll bet. I understand the cosmetology course like the one you're taking is quite time consuming and difficult. Are you learning anything from working part-time at Wanda's Beauty Salon?"

"A lot. It really helps to see in person what I'm reading about in the books. I'm so glad I could go to cosmetology school. I just love it, and I have you to thank for it."

"My pleasure. I'm just pleased I was able to help you with the financial part. As I told you before, pay me back when you can. I'm happy that you're still able to work here, although I know it's just a matter of time before I lose you permanently."

"I'll be here a few more months."

"Good. The customers really like you, and I know they're going to miss you."

"Well, everybody needs their hair cut, men and women, so they can come to Wanda's and see me," Madison said, smiling.

"To change the subject, how's your dad doing?"

"Great. It's been almost eight months now since he stopped drinking. We've really developed a close father-daughter relationship."

"That's wonderful. I know he consulted with Doc about his addiction to alcohol, but did he go to AA meetings or do anything else special?" Kelly asked.

"Yes, he's really active in AA, and I think it's good for him. He goes to a couple of meetings a week. Matter of fact, his favorite one is today at lunch time. They meet at the bank. Guess there's a room there the bank uses for staff meetings, and they let the AA group meet there once a week. Why?"

"I'd like to talk to your dad. Is he at home this morning?"

"Yes, it was too foggy this morning to take the boat out in the bay and fish. This talk of AA worries me, Kelly. You're not having a problem, are you?"

"No, honey. I just need a little information about the process for someone else, not for me. Would it be all right if I called your dad later this morning?"

"Of course. When it's foggy like this he usually goes back to bed, but he'll be up around 7:00. Any time after that would be fine."

A few hours later, Kelly said, "Roxie, I need to make a call. I'll be back in a few minutes."

"Hi Dave, this is Kelly Reynolds, formerly Kelly Conner. I'm the one who owns Kelly's Koffee Shop where Madison works."

"Of course, Kelly. I know who you are. By the way, I don't think I've ever properly thanked you for getting Doc to help me with my drinking problem. You know, I've been sober eight months now, and I feel the best I can ever remember. Believe it or not, the fish seem to know, and I'm catching a lot more of them than I ever did before. Life's pretty good, thanks to you!"

"I'm glad I was able to help. I've got a little favor to ask of you. I understand there's a man who attends AA meetings in the area who feels very strongly about people who own wine shops or liquor stores. I've heard that he says they're doing the devil's work. I'd like to know who he is, but I also know there's a code of anonymity among the people who attend the meetings."

"That's pretty much the main thing, Kelly. I don't know any of their last names. I do know the man you're talking about, and he rants constantly about liquor store owners, and how something should be done about them. Tell you what. I pretty much owe my life to you, so I feel like I owe you a favor. The guy will probably be at the AA meeting at the bank at noon today. We meet from 12:00 to 1:00 and I'm going to the meeting. Why don't you be on the sidewalk a few minutes before 1:00, and when we come out, I can gesture or whisper to you what the guy's wearing or something like that. Strictly speaking, that's not giving his name or identity away. Whatever you decide to do after that is your business."

"Dave, I really appreciate it. See you a few minutes before 1:00. Thanks."

She walked over to the cash register. "Roxie, I have an errand I have to do today. I need to leave about 12:45. It starts to slow down about that time anyway, and Madison's here to help. Okay with you if I take off then? I'm not sure if I'll be back."

"Sure, Kelly. Everything okay? You've never done this before."

"Yes. Everything's fine. I just need to check on something. Here's a spare key. If I'm not back, please lock up. Thanks."

Roxie took a long look at her. "Kelly, don't know what you're up to, but somehow I don't think Mike would be happy about it. Be careful, you hear?"

"Yes, ma'am. I promise I will." At 12:45 that afternoon, Kelly said, "Come on, Lady, let's go." They'd never before left the coffee shop prior to closing time. Lady sensed that something was definitely going on, and she wanted to be a part of it. She dutifully followed Kelly down the pier to the parking lot where they got in her minivan, Lady alert and ready for what she was sure would be a new adventure.

*****

Promptly at 1:00, Kelly stood a few feet down the sidewalk from the door of the bank. When several people started coming out at the same time, she was certain the AA meeting had ended. A deeply tanned tall, rangy man with blond sun-bleached hair walked over to her and said, "Kelly, it's good to see you again."

"Hi, Dave! You look absolutely great. I almost wouldn't have recognized you. I can see that the last eight months have definitely treated you well."

"They have indeed, thanks to you. Kelly, I think the person you're interested in is the man wearing the blue sweater who is just walking out now. And I probably should tell you he said at today's meeting it was about time someone took care of Jesse Allen, the owner of The Crush. I know he was the one who was recently murdered. Be careful."

"Don't worry, I will, and thanks, Dave." She turned away from him and crossed the street, watching the man in the blue sweater out of the corner of her eye. He walked to his car which was parked not too far from her minivan where Lady was patiently waiting for her. He started his car and drove to the highway that led out of town. Kelly followed at a discreet distance, staying three cars behind him. Her minivan was grey, and Mike always teased her that she'd never be given a ticket, because it was a thoroughly unmemorable car and cops look for more memorable cars. *Hope he's right*, she thought. *Hope the guy doesn't spot me.*

The man drove north from Cedar Bay for several miles then turned away from the ocean, driving up a gravel road. She saw a mailbox where the gravel road met the highway and read the name on it, "Richard Larson." She took out her phone and made a note on it with his name.

"Lady, think we'll go home early today. Need to do a little research on the computer, and it's probably better if Mike's not home when I do it."

She made a U-turn and headed back towards Cedar Bay.

*****

"Okay, Lady, time for me to get to work," Kelly said, heading down the hall to her home office where her computer was located, her footsteps clicking on the wooden floor. She knew she had a little time before Mike would be home, and she wanted to see what she could find out about Richard Larson. She booted up her computer and Googled Richard Larson. She quickly scanned the three pages where his name was mentioned and then went back to the beginning.

An hour later and after printing out several articles about him, she felt she had a pretty good sense of the man. He was forty-five years old, divorced, and a former insurance executive who had moved to the area from Seattle. Evidently the insurance company where he worked had let him go. He'd been arrested several times for driving under the influence and had even spent some time in jail. One article said that he'd had a revelation while he was in jail that alcohol was the root of all evil, and he'd vowed to wage a campaign to eliminate all liquor and wine stores in the State of Oregon. He traveled throughout the state, speaking to groups about the evils of alcohol. He was presently working for an insurance agent in Sunset Bay, but all of Beaver County was his territory. He'd been interviewed multiple times by members of the press regarding his attempts to have alcohol banned in Oregon. One of his interviewers had described him by using the terms "rabid" and "fanatical."

Kelly pushed herself away from the desk. *It's kind of like finding the*

.38 caliber gun and not being able to find out who pulled the trigger. This guy could have all the motives in the world for killing Jesse, and it looks like he does, but was he the one at the scene of the crime who fired the .38 that killed Jesse? That's the question that needs to be answered.

She heard Mike open the door and went to greet him. *Don't want to have to tell him any more fibs than necessary,* she thought, *and if he looked over my shoulder while I'm sitting in front of the computer, he'd probably want to know who the guy is, and this information about Richard Larson isn't quite ready for a prime time fireside chat just yet.*

CHAPTER FIFTEEN

"How goes the Jesse Allen case? Come up with any new information today?" Kelly asked when Mike joined her in the kitchen after changing out of his uniform.

"I did, but I'm just not sure what to make of it. First of all, I told you that Jesse was in debt, but I had no idea how bad it was. From going through his records yesterday and today, I found out he owed over $300,000. That's a lot of money to pay back, and on top of that it looks like The Crush has been losing money every month for the last year or so. I'm amazed he could even keep the doors open. He owned the building, so he didn't have to pay rent to a landlord, but I'm surprised his creditors didn't try to close him down. The only thing I can figure out is that any money he got in he shuffled around, first paying one creditor, and then another."

"Poor guy. That must have been horrible for him. He was so passionate about his wine and so knowledgeable. It's a shame he couldn't make a go of it. Now I feel guilty about his having brought us all the wine for our wedding and then he gave it to us at cost."

"I've been thinking the same thing. Normally I'd think suicide in a case where someone was that deeply in debt, but if he had commited suicide, the gun would have been in his hand and it wasn't, so I can rule that out."

"I would too, but like you said, there was definitely no gun in his hand." She opened the oven door and put the salmon they were going to have for dinner in it.

"Remember how I said last night that I was going to contact the local paper and television station and ask for help?"

"Yes."

"Well, the newspaper is probably just being delivered now, but the television station interviewed me on their noon broadcast. Part of the interview was how people could get in touch with me if they had information regarding the murder. This afternoon I got an anonymous call from a male individual. Usually anyone who calls with information in a murder case wants to remain anonymous, and this person told me he'd been driving by the rear of The Crush a little before the approximate time of the murder. I asked him if he'd noticed anything unusual. He told me he'd seen someone going into The Crush, but when I asked him if he could tell me if it was a man or a woman, he said no."

"That's interesting. What do you make of it?"

"I don't know. It could have just been a customer who saw Jesse going in and thought he was open for business. On the other hand, it could have been the killer. I asked him if the person he'd seen was small or large and if there was any kind of physical description he could give me. He said he wasn't paying that much attention, just that he'd noticed someone walking into the store. It doesn't really give me much information, but the fact that someone went into the store so close to the time of the murder might mean something."

"Have you established where the people who are on your list of possible suspects were at the time of murder?"

"No. That's what I'm going to do tomorrow. By the way, Roxie called me and said to tell you that she'd locked up and gotten everything ready for tomorrow. I asked her why you hadn't locked up, and she said you had an errand you had to run and that you never returned to the coffee shop after you left today. Is this something I should know about?" he asked, looking closely at her with an almost suspicious look on his face.

"No, not really," she said, quickly turning her back on him while she made the salad.

"Well, since we're married I think it would be nice if we trusted each other enough to tell the other one where we were when one of our business associates had to do something for us because we weren't available to do it. Something the spouse had always been able to do before. Seems to me that would kind of be an important thing to do in our marriage. What do you think?"

Lady barked, indicating she was ready for dinner. *Saved by the bark,* Kelly thought, sending a silent thank you to Lady. "Okay, girl, I know it's dinner time for you and Rebel. Give me just a minute."

As she poured some dog food into their dog dishes, she heard Mike say "This is Sheriff Mike," into his cell phone. Mike listened intently to what was being said. "I appreciate your call, sir, and if you can think of anything else, please don't hesitate to call me again."

"What was that all about?" she asked.

"The newspaper I told you about was delivered a little while ago, and the article about Jesse and my call for help to the community was on the front page. The man who just called said he was walking by The Crush on his way home from church, and he heard loud voices coming from inside the store. He said it sounded like people were arguing, but he couldn't tell whether it was a man's voice or a woman's voice."

"That would certainly fit in with the time frame of the murder. It almost had to be Jesse, but I wonder who he was arguing with."

"If I, and I repeat the word I, knew, I could probably solve the case. Now back to what we were discussing before the phone call. I won't force it, but I would like to know where you were this afternoon. Kelly, I love you, and I worry about you. Sometimes you go off half-cocked, and it could be dangerous for you. All of my instincts tell me your absence from the coffee shop was one of those times. Would I be right?"

"All right Mike, you got me. You're probably not going to be too happy about what I did, but you have to believe me when I tell you I was just trying to help you." She told him about calling Dave, the AA meeting, following Richard Larson, and finally researching him on the Internet.

For a long time Mike looked at her. "I don't know what to say. I can't believe you took such a risk. Honey, please, please, please don't do things like that. I'm scared to death something's going to happen to you. What if he is the one who murdered Jesse, and if he'd spotted you, who knows what might have happened? On the other hand, I have to give you credit for coming up with a pretty ingenuous plan for finding out the identity of this AA mystery man."

"See Mike, I've been telling you that you need me. I really can help you."

"Let me say a few things, and then let's talk about something else. I want the information you found out about the guy. I need to establish his whereabouts on the day of the murder. Secondly, I want you to keep the gun I bought you in your purse, and I want Lady with you at all times. If you can promise me you'll do that, I'll forget about what you did this afternoon, and I won't get angry."

"You have my word. Remember, it's not good to eat when you're angry, and you probably wouldn't enjoy dinner if you were. I promise you Mike, Lady and the gun will be with me from now on, but I don't know exactly what I should be frightened of."

"I don't either, but I just have a hunch you need to do those two things, and I've been in this game long enough to know that if I have a hunch about something, I better follow it. Deal?"

"Deal."

CHAPTER SIXTEEN

The coffee shop was just as busy as it had been during the previous two days. People wanted to find out what was happening in the murder case and commiserate about the crime wave that had descended on their sleepy little town of Cedar Bay.

I need to take a break, Kelly thought, walking into the kitchen to make sure Charlie had things ready for the lunchtime crowd. She went over to a chair in the corner that was there just for that purpose. She took her phone out of her purse, wanting to see if Mike had left a message for her.

No message from Mike, but this is interesting. There's a voicemail from Sophie this morning asking me to call her. I wonder what she wants. I probably should go out in front, but first I think I'll return her call. I'm curious.

"Good morning, Sophie, it's Kelly Conner, oops, Kelly Reynolds," she said when Sophie answered her phone. "I received your message to call you."

"That was fast. Thank you," Sophie said in her soft voice with a heavy French accent. "I've been debating about calling you, because I wanted to tell you a couple of things. I don't think very many people knew that Jesse owed money to his creditors. He was getting panicked about where he could find the money to pay them back. He told me they were making harassing calls to him day and night. I offered to loan him the money many times, but he wouldn't take my money. He told me that only weak men took money from women. He said I would think the only reason he was with me was because of my money. I didn't tell you this, but the morning he was killed we had a bitter argument over it. I went to see him at the store after church, and I told him his refusal to accept my offer was affecting our relationship. I could tell he was getting depressed, and I begged him to take my money. I have more than I need, but he refused. Now I wonder if someone killed him over some debt that he owed." Kelly heard her sobbing softly on the other end of the phone.

"Do you know if any of his creditors had ever threatened him? How did he deal with them when they called? Do you know if he borrowed money from individual people, or was it more that he owed companies that did business with him?"

"I don't know, Kelly. He didn't like to talk about it. I only found out when I overheard him talking to someone on the phone a few weeks ago. I asked him about the call, and that was when he told me he owed a lot of money. I asked him how much, and he told me it was around $300,000. I asked him if he had been sued or if people had tried to take his business from him. He said no, because as soon as he received any money, he would give some of it first to one creditor, then to another. He said it was getting harder and harder to juggle the money he received. That's all I know. Like I said, he didn't want to talk about it, and he wouldn't accept my money." Kelly heard her sigh and take a deep breath.

She continued, "When I left The Crush, he told me after the store closed that evening he would come to my house, and we would have dinner. As I drove away from the rear parking lot and turned the corner to drive home, I noticed someone going into his store."

"Did you recognize who it was?"

"No. I don't even know if it was a man or a woman. The only thing I remember is that they were bundled up in a hat and a coat. That's all I know."

"Thanks for calling, Sophie. I'll tell Mike. I'm sure he can find out who Jesse's major creditors were. How are you doing?"

"Well, to be honest, not so good. I really cared for him, and I'm so sad now that he's gone. Several of my friends here in Portland have been helping me get through this. They are trying to keep me busy by taking me out to lunch and dinner. My life has not been an easy one, and I've gotten through bad things before. I know I can do it again this time.

"One of my friends even volunteered to drive to my home on the coast and oversee a moving company load up everything in the house. I think I'll probably put most of the things that were in the house up for auction. It would be too painful for me to see things like the art glass that Jesse and I bought together. I've called a real estate agent, and the house will be put up for sale soon. I have to go, someone's at that door. *Au revoir,*" she said as she hung up the phone.

Yes, Kelly thought, *I think you will get through this. I imagine you're already looking to the future and letting go of the past, and who am I to judge? Au revoir. I don't want to think that you killed Jesse, but you certainly seem to be letting go of your grief awfully fast and selling the house and all the contents within it just days after Jesse's death. Gives a new meaning to the old slang saying, "Getting out of Dodge." Oh well, who knows how any of us would react in that situation?*

*****

"Okay, Lady, just a few more minutes, and we're out of here for the day," Kelly said, making sure everything had been turned off in the kitchen. She was just getting ready to turn off the lights when she heard the front door to the coffee shop open and saw Celia Parsons walking in.

"Hi, Celia, I'm closing up for the day, so I'm afraid I can't offer you anything. Sorry," she said, noticing Celia's eyes, shining like fiery coals, and her hair, unkempt and lank, plastered to her scalp.

Good grief. I'm not a psychologist, but I'd swear this woman looks like she's become unhinged. I wonder what's going on with her, Kelly thought.

"I didn't come here to eat. I came here to get your support for the Historical Society. You don't have a sign in the window showing that you're a member, and I checked and don't see where you've ever given any money to our organization."

"That's true. I don't have any extra time to donate to the Society, but I certainly support it. I think it's wonderful you're working hard to preserve the history of Cedar Bay."

"It's more than the history. The Society is about preserving a way of life. We consider what we have here in Cedar Bay precious, and we have to work hard to keep it that way. I was really happy that Jeff Black's son decided not to build that hotel and spa on his property last year after Jeff was killed. Who knows what would have happened if the riffraff that works at those places had come here? It's bad enough the Planning Commission granted a permit for Sophie Marchant to build that monstrosity of a house overlooking the bay. Best thing that could happen to this town is for that eyesore to burn down."

"Surely, you don't mean that. I agree it's not in keeping with most of the architectural styles here in Cedar Bay, but I'd hate for anything like that to happen."

"Well, if it did, it might keep that woman from ever coming back here. She didn't fool our members. We know when someone doesn't belong here, and we sure don't need any foreigners here, particularly some fancy French woman. Maybe it's a good thing my brother died. At least she won't have him as an excuse to stay here in Cedar Bay."

"I'm sorry, Celia, but I can't agree with you. One of the things that has made this town strong and come together in times of tragedy is because of the diversity we have in this community. I mean, look at the number of different church denominations we have. Certainly, you'd have to agree that the townspeople overall get along well with each other. It's unreasonable to expect that everyone would think and believe the same way. No, if someone is an honest citizen who adds to the community, rather than taking from it, I think there's a place for that person here in Cedar Bay. You may not agree, and that's your right, just like it's the right of other people to live as they wish."

"So are you telling me you won't support the Historical Society? Even if you can't donate your time, you can donate some of your money. A lot of your customers do, and they'd probably like to see a sign in your window showing that you support the Historical Society. Be a shame if something happened to you or this crummy little hole-in-the-wall coffee shop of yours, considering how long it's been around," Celia said in a threatening tone of voice that was rising in intensity as she spoke.

Lady sensed that something was wrong and walked over to Kelly, facing Celia, a low growl coming from her throat. "Lady, hush," Kelly said. "Celia, it's been nice talking to you. I have an appointment, and I don't want to be late. You'll have to leave now."

"Fine. Don't say I didn't warn you," she said, turning around so quickly her purse flew open, and several things fell out of it and onto the floor. Kelly stooped down to help her pick them up.

That's weird. Her business card says "Cedar Bay Historical Society – Established in 1907." I'd swear I've seen something recently that kind of looked like the logo on her card, but for the life of me I can't remember what it was or where I saw it.

"Here you are, Celia," she said, handing the items she'd picked up to Celia. "I'll think about what you said and let you know. Thanks for stopping by. Lady, come."

Celia strode down the pier, not bothering to thank Kelly for helping her pick up what she'd spilled out of her purse.

I can't think of two siblings more different from each other. Jesse was one of the nicest people I've ever met, and Celia's not only one of the most abrasive people I've ever met, I'm beginning to think she's deranged. Maybe it's a good thing for Sophie that she won't be marrying Jesse. I can't imagine having a worse sister-in-law.

CHAPTER SEVENTEEN

The next morning when he arrived at his office, Mike said to Angie, his longtime secretary, "Would you hold my calls? I want to do some research this morning, and I need to be able to concentrate."

"Sure, Mike. By the way, you know Tony, my husband. He feels real bad about Jesse's murder. He told me Jesse always took a lot of time with him when he went in The Crush to get wine. He was wondering if you have any leads in his murder."

"I've got some people I think might qualify as potential suspects, but nothing I'd take to the bank. The killer's out there, but it's not easy finding him or her. I feel like I'm getting closer, you know, kind of like that kid's game – you're getting warmer when you're about to guess the right answer. I think I'm getting warmer. Tell him when I get hot, I'll let everybody know."

She laughed. "I haven't thought of that game for years. When I was in my last month of my pregnancy with Susie, Tony and I used to play it at night when I couldn't sleep. I don't think I've played it or even thought about it since then. I'll tell him what you said."

Mike and Rebel walked into his office and he closed the door behind them. "Okay boy, you might as well get comfortable. This might take awhile." One hour later, having done a lot of research on his computer, he was able to get the name of the insurance agency where Richard Larson worked in Sunset Bay. He dialed the number he'd found for it.

"Hello. Triple A Insurance Agency. How may I direct your call?" the receptionist asked.

"This is Sheriff Mike Reynolds. I'd like to speak to the manager."

"That would be Derek Martinez. Please hold. I'll see if he's available."

Within moments, a man's voice said, "This is Derek Martinez, Sheriff. How can I help you?"

"Well, I'm not real sure. I'm calling about one of your employees, a man by the name of Richard Larson. I'd appreciate any information you could give me about him."

"When Judy told me you were on the phone, I was pretty sure it would be about Richard. Here's the thing, Sheriff. My wife is a recovering alcoholic, and she met Richard at an AA meeting. He told her he'd been a high ranking executive with an insurance company in Seattle, but because of his problems with alcohol, he was fired. He'd visited this area on vacation once and had good memories of it, so he decided to come here, start over, and look for a job. My wife suggested I hire him, and even though I knew I was taking a chance, I did. He's a very charming and charismatic man and a darned good insurance salesman when he's sober."

"I gather from that statement he's still having trouble with alcohol."

"That might be the understatement of the year. His wife divorced him, and as I told you, he was fired from his job in Seattle. You'd think that would be enough to make anyone turn their life around, but he's only successful about half the time. It seems he's either drunk and can't work, or when he isn't drunk he's going to every AA meeting around these parts. He's always talking about how alcohol should be illegal in the State of Oregon, and how something should be done about the people who sell alcohol. I think in some twisted way he blames the people who sell alcohol for his alcoholism."

"It seems like a stretch, but I suppose there's a shred of sense in that thinking."

"You're a far more generous man than I am, Sheriff. If it wasn't for my wife, I would have fired him long ago, although occasionally he does bring in a good client. It's a very frustrating situation."

"I can well imagine. Have you ever known him to threaten a liquor store owner?"

"Yes. There's a liquor store here in Sunset Bay where he used to buy his liquor. In one of his sober moments, he threatened to kill the owner if he didn't close the liquor store. I think he said something about it being the work of the devil. The liquor store owner called me and complained. There really wasn't much I could do but talk to Richard. He promised it would never happen again, but he was permanently refused service at that store. Occasionally he still goes on a bender and no one hears from him for a couple of days, then he goes back to attending all the AA meetings in the area. I know he really wants to quit permanently, but he can't seem to do it. Now that I've told you what I know about him, may I ask why you're calling?"

"A man who owned a wine store in Cedar Bay was recently murdered. I'm looking for any tie-ins. Someone told me that Richard had talked in a very negative way about liquor store owners, so I thought I'd follow up on it."

"I remember hearing about that murder on television. I think you were being interviewed about it. Richard lives on the outskirts of Cedar Bay. I've never been to his home, but you might want to talk to him there. I've learned from being in the insurance business for many years that you can get a real sense of the person when you're on their turf. Would you like his address?"

"Thanks, Derek, I already have it. I really appreciate your help. If I find out anything, I'll let you know, and if you think of anything else or hear something, I'd appreciate it if you'd call me."

"Happy to, Sheriff. It's been nice talking to you."

Mike walked out to Angie's desk. "I'm going to leave for a couple of hours. Anything important come up while I was doing some research?"

"Nothing that can't wait until you get back. Lem, the attorney, called. He's back in town from his vacation and wants to talk to you about Jesse and some legal issues. I told him you were doing some research, and he said it was probably just as well you were busy, because he's got a lot of catching up to do after taking off for a few days."

"Okay, we'll be back in a couple of hours. Come on Rebel, let's go talk to this guy and see what we can find out."

Typical January weather, Mike thought on the drive to Richard Larson's ranchette, *grey and misty, chilly but not cold. Think everybody here in the Pacific Northwest lives for the next time they'll see some sun. This has been going on for a long time now, and everyone's getting pretty tired of it. Maybe that's why we treasure the few days we have here on the coast that are warm and sunny. Probably why Richard Larson decided to move here. Be willing to bet when he came here to visit it was warm and sunny. No one told the poor guy that a day or two like that is pretty rare.*

After a short drive out of town on the main highway, Mike saw the Larson mailbox and turned up the gravel road that led to Richard's modest ranchette home. It didn't look like he was at home and no car was in the driveway. The house was badly in need of repair. Paint was flaking off of the shutters, weeds were on either side of the sidewalk leading up to the house, and it practically screamed out the word "neglect."

Rebel jumped out of the patrol car and followed Mike up to the front door. Mike looked down at Rebel and saw that his hackles were raised. He wasn't growling or barking, but there was no mistaking the tension in him, as if he were prepared for some sort of danger. Mike rang the bell and also knocked on the door. *With the way this property's been neglected, I'd be willing to bet the doorbell's broken.* He waited several minutes, and no one came to the door.

"Come on Rebs, let's walk around the house. Maybe we can peek inside." He stepped off the porch and walked around to a window on the side of the house. Mike stood on his tiptoes and looked into the kitchen.

Good grief, I've never seen anything like this. He stood in shock, surveying the empty vodka and beer bottles that completely covered the countertop along with empty cans of food and a half-eaten sack of potato chips. He took his phone out its holster and snapped some pictures. Rebel stood as close to him as possible, trembling.

"It's okay, Rebel. Come." Mike walked around to the rear of the house where a trash can overflowed with more empty beer and vodka bottles along with all kinds of fast food wrappers and containers. "He may be trying to get off of the stuff, but from what I'm seeing, it's definitely winning the battle, and he's losing it."

There were no drapes or other types of window coverings, and Mike was able to easily look through the sliding glass door at what he assumed was the family room. He saw a large television set in the corner. Mike took a deep breath and stared, speechless, at the numerous hand-painted posters filled with hateful words and directed toward the liquor industry that were tacked up on the wall. "Death To The Booze Pushers," "The Only Good Liquor Store Owner Is A Dead Liquor Store Owner," and "Burn, Baby, Burn The Liquor Stores," were only a few of the posters he saw on the walls.

He took more pictures and continued around the house to what looked like a bedroom. In stark contrast to what he had seen in the other rooms, the bedroom was very neat. The bed was made, and there was a large sign above the bed that read, "The Big Book." On the dresser was a well-thumbed copy of the book that members of AA considered to be their Bible.

I've never seen anything like this. The poor guy, I mean I have to feel sorry for him, he has got to be living his life in some sort of a horrible seesaw battle. The demons of alcohol are certainly snapping at his heels. Looks like part of him gives in to his urges, and the other part tries to fight them. I have no idea whether or not he's the killer, but it sure looks like he might be capable of it if he'd been drinking and blamed Jesse for his problems because he sold alcohol. That's pretty perverted thinking, but anyone who commits murder probably thinks in a perverted way.

Mike and Rebel walked back to his patrol car, Rebel visibly more relaxed than he had been. "Come on, Rebs, let's go call Lem. Don't know what I was expecting to find here, but this certainly wasn't on my radar. Wow! This place is like something out of a movie. You'd have to see it to believe it."

CHAPTER EIGHTEEN

"We're back, Angie. I gotta tell you, I'm ready for the sun to peep through the overcast. This grey mist is getting old. I've always heard Seattle has the highest suicide rate in the country because of all the rain up there, but if this keeps up, we might give them a run for their money."

"I certainly hope not. With all the murders we've had in the last year, we sure don't need something like a suicide epidemic."

"You're right. Got anything new for me?"

"Yes. A man by the name of John Baker called and would like you to call him."

"Did he say what it was regarding?"

"No. Here's his number. You know if it's about a case or something like that, they usually won't tell me much. It was that kind of a conversation."

"Thanks. I'll give him a call and see what he wants."

A few minutes later after he'd given Rebel a fresh bowl of water and a treat, he dialed the number Angie had given him.

"May I speak with John Baker? This is Sheriff Reynolds."

"This is John," the voice on the other end said. "Thanks for getting back to me so promptly."

"No problem. What can I do for you?"

"Well, Sheriff. I'd like this conversation to be confidential. In other words, I don't want anyone to know that I called you, or what I'm calling about. I'd appreciate it if you do something with the information I'm going to give you, that there won't be any reference to me. Would you agree to that?"

"I haven't heard what you're going to tell me, so I'm a little reluctant to promise you that in advance, but yes, I probably can."

The man took a deep breath and began to speak. "I'm the controller for the Pellino Brothers Vineyard, and I'm very concerned about some things that have been happening around here. For instance, in the last two weeks alone, over five million dollars has been deposited into the company's bank account from an unidentified account in the Cayman Islands."

Mike let out a low whistle. "That's a lot of money. Has that ever happened before?"

"No. I overheard the brothers talking about wanting to buy the White Cloud Retreat Center vineyard that's adjacent to their vineyard. They didn't know I could hear them. Dante told Luca that it was a good thing the Allen guy was dead. He said he thought it was just a matter of time before Luke Monroe, the owner of the White Cloud Retreat Center, would realize he couldn't run the vineyard without some help, and therefore he'd be inclined to sell it to them. Luca told him maybe it was time to do something to hasten the process."

"That sounds a little ominous. Did he say anything specific?"

"No, but there was a guy here from Chicago for the last week or so by the name of Guido Salerno. He left just a couple of days ago, but between you and me, he gave me the willies, and I think he scared the brothers, too. He was also here a couple of months ago. I hate to sound prejudiced, but if I was ever going to pick a guy who looked like he was a Mafia hit man, he'd be the guy I'd pick, hands down, no contest. Before Guido went back to Chicago, I overheard Luca tell Dante that he wished Guido would just get it over with and leave."

"Are you telling me you think Luke's life could be in danger?"

"Sheriff, I honestly don't know. I've worked for the brothers for several years, and while they pay me well, I can't say that I like them. I don't think they're good men, if you know what I mean. I wouldn't put anything past them, but I don't have any solid proof to back it up. The one thing I do know is that they want the land that the Center owns in a big way. And from my experience with them, they usually get what they want."

"Why do you think they're so focused on that particular property? I mean, there's a lot of other land around here they could use to grow grapes on."

"They want to make a pinot noir that's as good as Scott Monroe made when he was alive. He grew the grapes for his wine on that property, so I think they feel if they can get that land, they can make an award winning pinot noir just like he did. Hate to say this, because I have absolutely no basis for it, but it's kind of ironic that originally they hoped to buy the property because they didn't think Luke knew what he was doing. Then Luke hired Jesse Allen to help him, and now Allen's been murdered. I've got no proof of any tie-in, but I sure think it's kind of interesting."

"Yeah, so do I. Got anything else for me?" Mike asked.

"No. I just thought you might be interested in what I've observed here at the vineyard."

"Thanks John, I appreciate you taking the time to call me. Do me a favor. If you see or hear anything else that you think might be important for me to know, don't hesitate to call. I promise you I won't divulge your identity or what you've told me."

"Will do, Sheriff. If I hear anything else, I'll definitely let you know."

Mike buzzed Angie. "Hold my calls for an hour or so. I've got a little more research I need to do. For the next hour he read everything he could find on the Internet about Guido Salerno and the Pellino brothers. He finally sat back in his chair, troubled by what he'd found out about the three of them.

So Guido Salerno was tried for murder in New Jersey, he thought as he doodled on the piece of paper in front of him. *The newspaper clippings said that it was a classic type of Mafia contract murder. The District Attorney couldn't prove his case, and Guido got off because of a hung jury. Both of the Pellino brothers were arrested numerous times for extortion, money laundering, and other white collar crimes when they lived in Chicago. Their names were tied several times to a man named Angelo Rossi, who it turns out, has well-known Mafia connections in Chicago.*

Confidential tax records of the IRS, available only to law enforcement authorities, indicate the IRS thinks Rossi and the Chicago Mafia are the secret owners of the Pellino Brothers Vineyard, but they haven't been able to prove it. Guido Salerno moved from the New Jersey area to Chicago and now allegedly works for Rossi as an enforcer.

Guido and the Pellino brothers certainly qualify as suspects. Maybe Rossi sent Guido out to get rid of Jesse. If he is a Mafia hired gun and if the Pellino brothers are Mafia, it makes perfect sense that Guido would stay at their vineyard. It's also interesting that he returned to Chicago immediately after Jesse's death.

All this makes me concerned about Luke's safety. I suppose the good news is that this guy Guido has left, but based on what I've just read, the Pellino brothers might be capable of killing Luke. Sounds like they're willing to do about anything to get the White Cloud property.

He found Luke's number and called it. "Hi Luke, it's Sheriff Mike. I don't want to alarm you, but I've received some confidential information that makes me concerned for your safety. It may be nothing, but I'd feel better if I knew you were taking some safety precautions, like keeping a gun near you."

"That's great, Mike. Just the call everyone wants to get from their sheriff. A call alerting them that they might be in danger. As a matter of fact your wife also cautioned me to keep a gun with me at all times, so I have one right next to me as we speak."

"Like I said, it may be nothing, but I kind of remember something that Benjamin Franklin said about an ounce of prevention is worth a pound of cure. Think it might be appropriate here. In other words, I'd rather have you avoid a problem than try to fix it later on or worse yet, have me try to fix it."

"Thanks for calling. I'll be very careful, so you won't have to fix any problems concerning me."

"Good. Hate to have anything happen to my wife's favorite yoga teacher. Talk to you later."

CHAPTER NINETEEN

Angie buzzed Mike just after he'd ended the call with Luke.

"Mike, sorry to bother you, but Lem's on line one. He says he'd really like to talk to you if you have a few minutes."

"Thanks, I'll take the call."

"Good afternoon, Lem, how was your vacation?"

"As always, way too short, but we really had a good time. We left right after your wedding and went up to Seattle for a couple of days. Love that town! My wife's a big Dale Chihuly fan. He's the guy who does all the art glass stuff. His pieces are pretty incredible, and he's got exhibitions all over the world. Fascinating stuff. Wish we could afford a piece of his work. I think my wife's one regret in life is that she never bought a piece of his years ago when she was a student at the University of Washington, and he was selling his art glass out of the trunk of his car. If she had, I could probably retire."

"Kind of rings a bell, but I'm not familiar with him, or for that matter, anybody in the art world. It's one of the things I never got around to learning about," Mike said.

"He's got a permanent exhibition in the Tacoma Art Museum. We stopped there on our way up to Seattle, and there was also a special show of his blown glass pieces at the Seattle Art Museum. Take a minute and look him up on the Internet. I think you'll like his work. Some of his pieces are huge, I'm talking twenty feet tall, or more. It's amazing! You look at his stuff, and you can't figure out how anyone could blow glass and make those huge pieces. It's kind of ironic he was blinded in one eye by glass, but it wasn't from blowing glass. He was in an automobile accident, and it was from the windshield."

"Next time I go to Seattle I'll check it out. I know Kelly loves things like that. We didn't take a honeymoon, and the stay at-home and relax honeymoon we were planning only lasted about half a day, until we found Jesse Allen's body. When this case is solved, might be time for a belated honeymoon."

"That's why I'm calling. I have some information for you about Jesse. My poor secretary says that Jesse's ex-wife Sydney is driving her nuts. She says Sydney must have called twenty times a day for the last two days, to see if I'd checked in with my secretary while I was gone."

"What was she calling about?"

"This is kind of a dicey situation. Jesse had a large life insurance policy he took out when he was married to Sydney. They agreed he wouldn't have to pay her alimony since she was a school principal and had a fairly nice income, but instead he would keep her on as the primary beneficiary on his life insurance policy in case something happened to him."

"Can't blame her for calling. She probably wants to get that money sooner rather than later."

"That's the dicey part. She's not going to get the money."

Mike interrupted him. "What are you talking about? When I was going through Jesse's files, I found his life insurance policy, and Sydney was named as the primary beneficiary."

"Correction, Mike. You saw the old insurance policy. Early last week Jesse made an appointment with me. He told me he was deeply in debt and couldn't remember when I handled the divorce for him if he'd signed anything that meant he had to keep Sydney on as the primary beneficiary of the one million dollar policy. I told him no, that it was a gentleman's agreement between the two of them and not legally enforceable. Bottom line is he decided he didn't want to play nice and be a gentleman any longer."

"What do you mean?"

"I mean that Jesse changed the person named as the primary beneficiary of the policy from Sydney to me with the stipulation the proceeds from the policy were to only be used to pay off his creditors. In other words, Sydney is no longer a beneficiary, and she gets nothing."

"Have you told her?"

"No. I wanted to talk to you first. I know she's going to be furious when I tell her, and quite frankly, she can be a hothead at times. The reason I called is to ask you if you could possibly come to my office at 4:30 today. She has an appointment with me then, and I'm going to have to tell her about the change in the life insurance policy."

"Sounds like what you want me to do is sit there and keep my gun in my hand in case she pulls one out."

"Yeah, and you might also remember she won the pistol shooting competition at the county fair a few years ago. I've never known her to be violent, but I don't want to find out the hard way."

"I'll be there to make sure she doesn't do anything she might regret."

"I'm the one who might regret it if she does anything," Lem chuckled.

"One more question, Lem. Do you know if Sydney knows that Jesse changed the beneficiary designation on the insurance policy?"

"No, I don't. I'd have a hard time believing he would have told her knowing their stormy past and her temper, but maybe she found out. Maybe that's why she's been calling so much, to see if what she heard is true. I have a hunch you're thinking that if she found out about it, it might have provided a pretty good motive for her to kill him."

"Unfortunately, that's exactly what I was thinking. Well, we should know more this afternoon. See you then."

Mike buzzed Angie. "I'm going to have to leave early today. I have a meeting over at Lem's office at 4:30. I'll go home after that."

"No problem. By the way, the state police DNA lab called. Want me to get them on the line for you?"

"Give me about five minutes. I need to call Kelly and tell her I might be a little late for dinner."

He called Kelly on her cell phone. "Hi, sweetheart, how is Mrs. Reynolds doing this afternoon?"

"Mrs. Reynolds is fine, thank you. I'm just pulling out of the market. Plan on pork chops stuffed with blue cheese and artichoke hearts along with a killer sauce when you get home."

"I wish I was on the way right now. There's a meeting I have to attend, so I may be a little late tonight. Hope that doesn't ruin your menu."

"No, I won't even start until you get here. Take your time. Anything happen of interest today?"

"Yeah, a lot. I'll tell you all about it when I get home. Loves!"

He looked down at the phone and saw that line two was blinking. He buzzed Angie. "Angie, I see there's a call on line two. Is that the state police lab?"

"Yes, they're on hold for you."

"Thanks," he said, punching line two on his phone. "This is

Sheriff Reynolds, may I help you?"

A few minutes later he hung up, wondering how the information he'd received from the state police lab was going to affect his and Kelly's lives.

CHAPTER TWENTY

At 4:25 Mike walked into Lem's law office and saw Sydney sitting in the waiting room. "Good afternoon, Sydney, how are you?"

"I've been better. I'm glad Lem's back in town, because I really need to talk to him. What are you doing here?"

Before Mike could respond, the door to Lem's office opened, and he walked out into the reception room. "Sydney, Mike, it's good to see both of you. Please come into my office. Would you like some coffee or water?"

"No thanks," they both said simultaneously. Sydney sat down in one of the two client chairs located on the opposite side of the oak desk from where Lem was seated. Mike sat on the brown leather couch behind Lem's desk.

"Lem, why is Mike here? I asked to meet with you, not him. I expected to have a private and personal meeting with you. What we talk about is none of the sheriff's business."

"This meeting regards a person who is now deceased. Since Mike is investigating his murder, I thought it was appropriate for him to be here. You aren't my client, your ex-husband was, so there's no violation of an attorney-client relationship."

"Well, if you want him here, it's your law office," she said scowling at Mike. She turned back to Lem. "I want to know when I'll get the proceeds from the life insurance policy Jesse had naming me as his primary beneficiary. I don't know who the executor of Jesse's will is, but since you're his attorney, and neither his mother nor sister ever said anything to me about it, I'm assuming it's you."

"That's right, Sydney, I'm the executor of his estate, and as such, I have to tell you that you won't be getting any proceeds from the insurance policy."

"What are you talking about? Jesse and I had an agreement," she said, jumping up from her chair and raising her voice. "That was part of our divorce settlement. He was to name me as the primary beneficiary on his life insurance policy. You know that."

"Sit down. What you're saying is true. At the time you were divorced, Jesse named you as the primary beneficiary on his life insurance policy, but you may remember that there was no written agreement about it. It was only an unenforceable oral agreement. Early last week Jesse changed his mind. He was deeply in debt, and named me as the primary beneficiary of the policy with the caveat being that if he died, I was to distribute the proceeds from the insurance policy to his creditors. The balance of the proceeds are to be given to The Wine Institute of Oregon to be used for educational purposes."

"He can't do that! We had an agreement. So what if he was in debt? That doesn't have anything to do with me!" she screamed as her face turned red with anger.

"Please lower your voice, Sydney. You're absolutely right. If you had been the recipient of the policy proceeds, you would not be legally bound to distribute any of that money to his creditors, however, that's not the case. I will be the recipient of the policy proceeds. Here's a copy of the legal document Jesse signed, instructing me how to distribute the proceeds. This copy is for you. The original will be part of the documents I'll be filing with the probate court tomorrow."

Sydney stared at Lem in disbelief as her shaking hand snatched the piece of paper he handed her, her gold bracelets jangling. She quickly read it and stood up.

"You're just as slippery as he was. I'll have my attorney look at this, and the next time I see you will be in court when I sue you for the proceeds from that policy." She flounced out the door, slamming it behind her.

Lem sat back down in his chair. "I thought that went well, didn't you?" he asked Mike sarcastically.

"Well, the good news is that she didn't pull a gun on you. Can she sue you over that document Jesse signed?"

"You're right about the gun and yes, she could sue me. You can sue anybody for anything, but the question is 'does she have a case?' Any honest lawyer knows she'd lose in a court of law, however there are a lot of unethical lawyers around who might tell her she could possibly win while they make her pay a fat retainer and bill her at an outrageous hourly rate. It could end up costing her a lot of money, and she'd still lose her case."

"She's a big girl. That's a decision she'll have to make. What I find interesting is that she certainly seemed shocked by what you just told her. If she knew about the change in beneficiaries before she came in here, she's one heck of an actress."

Lem took off his tortoiseshell rimmed glasses and rubbed his eyes. "I agree. You said you saw an insurance policy in his files naming her as the beneficiary. Where did you find it?"

"It was in his desk in the small office he had at The Crush. Why?"

"Pretty far out thought, but what if she'd seen that policy recently and knew he was getting farther and farther into debt? He may have even told her he was sinking financially and about to go broke. If someone needed to cut their expenses, what's one of the first things they'd do? They'd cancel their life insurance policy. I'm not saying she's the one who shot poor Jesse, but it certainly is food for thought. Perhaps she was afraid he'd cancel the policy and she'd never get any money from him, so she figures it's better to kill him while he still has the policy in full force and effect."

"Next time you're looking for work, Lem, let me know. Think I could use you over at my office. That's a pretty interesting theory. I need to mull it over."

They both stood up. "Mike, thanks for coming on such short notice. Fortunately you didn't have to do any lawman stuff or pull out your gun, but I felt better knowing you had my back covered, literally, from where you were sitting."

"You've got a permit to carry a gun, don't you, Lem?"

"Yes, but I've never found it necessary to carry a concealed weapon. My wife made me get a permit to carry one several years ago when I was representing a wife in a messy divorce case, and the husband threatened to kill me. Why do you ask?"

"I kind of remember issuing the permit to you. Given that you're the bad guy in Sydney's eyes, might be a good thing for you to keep a gun near you, like in your desk, in your car, or by your nightstand. I'm sure you won't have to use it, but I'd feel better if you had it handy."

"Thanks. That's enough to make anybody's day – have the sheriff tell you he thinks you need to keep a gun near you. Okay, I will, but I'm not particularly happy about it."

"I'm sure you won't need it, but it's been my experience when people are prepared for things, they don't get caught off guard and get themselves hurt or worse yet, get themselves killed."

"Consider it done. Tell Kelly hi and that she was a beautiful bride. We thought it was a nice touch to have Cash and Julia in the wedding. Gotta tell you, from where I was sitting, I could see a lot of handkerchiefs brushing away tears. Again, congratulations."

"Well, Lem, you have a good evening," Mike said, as he put on his signature white Stetson hat and gave him a mock salute. He walked out the door to the patrol car where Rebel was patiently waiting for him, standing up in the front seat and making sure the car was just as Mike had left it when he went into Lem's office.

CHAPTER TWENTY-ONE

"We're home," Mike said, as he walked into the house, Rebel faithfully following at his heels. He saw Kelly in the kitchen getting things out of the refrigerator.

"Hey beautiful, I am so glad to see you after the day I've had." He walked over to her, put his arms around her, and kissed the back of her neck.

"Sheriff Mike, you keep that up, and dinner will be delayed," she said laughingly. "Actually, keep the thought, but I've got a lot to tell you, and I imagine you have a lot to tell me, according to Angie."

"Angie? When did you talk to her?"

"When I couldn't reach you on your cell phone. I had a weird visit from Celia today at the coffee shop, and I was calling to tell you about it. When we'd talked earlier, you sounded frazzled, so I didn't go into it. Angie said you'd been busy from the time you got to the office, and you'd already left for an appointment you had with Lem. What's up with that?"

"Let me feed the dogs and change out of my uniform. I'm getting the evil eye from both of them. You could pour me a glass of wine, and I'll tell you in a minute. Can you hold dinner for a little while?"

"Absolutely. Actually, I think I'll make a fire in the fireplace. Perfect night for one."

"Here you go, sheriff. Enjoy," she said, handing him a glass of wine a few minutes later.

"It's good, Kelly," he said, taking a sip, "but I have to tell you the White Cloud Pinot Noir that Scott produced was better. That's somewhat related to one of the things that happened today. I got a call from someone who's working at the Pellino Brothers Vineyard." He told her about the conversation he'd had with John Baker, but true to his promise to John, never mentioned his name. He also mentioned he'd called Luke, and expressed his concern about his safety.

"Like they say in the television ads, but wait, that's not all, there's more. Remember the guy you followed, the one from the AA meeting?"

"Yes, of course. I could hardly forget him. Actually, I've been thinking a lot about him."

"I had a long conversation with his employer this morning, and I went out to his house. Here are a couple of photos I took while I was there. It was really bizarre. I've never seen anything quite like it before," he said reaching for his phone.

"Good grief, Mike. On one hand he seems to be a raging alcoholic, and on the other, a man desperate to get sober. Talk about a split personality. What did his employer have to say about him?"

He told her the gist of his conversation with Derek. "And that's not all. I met with Lem and Jesse's ex-wife, Sydney."

"Sounds like you really did get around a lot today. How is Sydney doing and why the meeting with Lem? I thought he'd been Jesse's lawyer when the two of them got divorced."

"He was, but seems like things aren't quite what they appear to be."

"That sounds rather cryptic. What do you mean?"

He told her about the meeting and how he'd become concerned about Lem's personal safety, because Sydney had a reputation as a hothead and was a crack shot. He went on to tell her how shocked Sydney seemed to be when Lem said she was no longer the primary beneficiary on Jesse's insurance policy.

"Wow, I bet she wasn't expecting that. So now you have the Pellino brothers, who have always been on your radar, a hit man from Chicago, a disgruntled ex-wife who's a crack shot and just found out that she's not the beneficiary of a large insurance policy, and a sometimes recovering alcoholic who hates liquor store owners. Those are all people who definitely might qualify as suspects. Let me give you another one, Celia Parsons, Jesse's sister."

"What made you think of her?"

"I mentioned to you she came to the coffee shop today. I knew she was the president of the Historical Society, and I knew she didn't like Sophie Marchant, but I'm not so sure she couldn't be the one who killed Jesse. She's absolutely rabid on the subject of keeping foreigners out of Cedar Bay. Remember her mother told me that Jesse said he was going to marry Sophie. As hard as it is to believe, she may have killed her brother to keep Cedar Bay pure. If that's not downright twisted thinking, I don't know what is. After I met with her today, I had the sense she could almost qualify as being deranged." She related the details of Celia's visit to the coffee shop and how she looked and acted.

"All right. I've heard enough. That was definitely a threat, and from what you told me, Lady sure sensed it, too. Remember your promise to me. From now on, you and the gun I got you are going to be inseparable. You don't go anywhere without it, and while we're on the subject, I want you to take Lady with you everywhere you go until this thing is solved. You're the third person today I've had to tell to keep a gun near them. This case is definitely heating up. We've got some people involved in this case who are having a difficult time dealing with reality, and I don't want you mistaken for being the cause of their troubles if they spin out of control and sink into one of their unreal worlds.

Mike's phone started buzzing and he looked at the monitor. "It's the fire marshal. I need to take his call." He listened for a few minutes and ended the call. "As if things couldn't get any worse, Sophie's house is on fire. The county fire marshal just issued a call for all volunteer firemen from the surrounding area to respond to the scene of the fire. He wants me out there ASAP to provide security and crowd control. I don't like what I'm thinking, and I imagine you're thinking the same thing. This is a little too coincidental. I have to go out to Sophie's house right now, but I was saving the best news for last," he said smiling as he stood up.

"I told you I wasn't going to get involved in the DNA test Julia called you about, but I had second thoughts about it and had the samples couriered to the state police DNA lab. Julia's fiancé, Brad, is definitely the father of the two girls. That should make all of them happy. I was going to tell you all about it, and I'd planned on the two of us calling her with the good news tonight, but given this turn of events, I'd appreciate it if you'd call her. Tell her she can call me at the office tomorrow if she needs particulars, but it was a definite match with no room for error."

"Mike, that's the best news I've heard in quite awhile. I'm so happy for all of them."

"I've got to go, and I'll take Rebel with me. Keep Lady and the gun with you. Like I said, seems like things are accelerating rather quickly in this case."

"I'll leave your dinner in the refrigerator with instructions how to cook it on the counter, and I'll leave the light on over the stove, so you'll know I've gone to bed. I wonder if anyone has called Sophie about the fire yet," she said, following Mike down the hall as he got ready to change back into his uniform. "She called me today and told me she and Jesse had argued the morning of his death because he wouldn't accept money from her to pay off his creditors. She thought I should know and didn't want me to hear it from someone else."

"Kelly, I'm reluctant to ask this of you, but you seem to have a better rapport with her than anyone else does. Any chance you could call her for me? She'd probably take finding out about the fire better from you than from me or someone else."

"Sure, I can do that. See you later. Be safe!" she said as he walked out the door with Rebel at his side.

CHAPTER TWENTY-TWO

"Hi, Mom," Julia said when she answered Kelly's phone call. "How's the old married lady?"

"Doing well, considering it hasn't even been a week, but it sure has been busy around here. The number of suspects in Jesse's case is growing by leaps and bounds, and Mike's insisting I keep my gun and Lady with me at all times. From that, you can assume he thinks he's getting close to figuring out who killed Jesse."

"Your gun? Mom, I didn't know you had a gun!"

"I do now. Mike bought it for me almost a year ago and took me out to the gun range, so I'd get comfortable with it. I rarely ever carry it, although in the last few cases he's had, I've gotten into a couple of situations where it sure helped my comfort level."

"That's just swell. Sure doesn't help my comfort level to hear that. I thought Rebel was providing all the comfort level you needed."

"Well, when you were here, I think I mentioned that Rebel was getting quite attached to Mike. Actually, the more I think about it, I'm certain Mike got Lady for me, because Rebel was shifting his loyalty to Mike. I'm also pretty sure he's a lot more liberal with treats for Rebel than I've ever been. That may be part of the attraction, but Lady is turning out to be every bit as protective of me as Rebel.

Anyway, that's not why I called."

"Okay, I'll bite. Out with it."

"Are you sitting down?" Kelly asked.

"Yes, but you've definitely affected my comfort level with those words."

"Darling, I have some wonderful news for you and believe me, your comfort level is going to be just fine."

"Mom, hurry up. You're killing me with the suspense."

"Mike sent the hair samples by courier to the state police lab. He got the results back today. Brad is definitely the girls' father. The test was one hundred percent conclusive."

Julia was silent for a few moments, and then Kelly heard her crying softly into the phone. "Oh, Mom, you'll never know what those words mean to me," she said tearfully. "He's such a wonderful man. I can't wait for you to meet both him and my stepdaughters-to-be. Hate to tell you this, but you're going to be an instant step grandmother."

"Well, I'd appreciate it if you'd at least send me pictures of my future son-in-law and the two girls. When do I get to meet them?"

"We were talking about it last night, and we're kind of planning on driving up to Cedar Bay around Easter. Brad and I can both take some time off from our jobs around then. How would that work for you?"

"Absolutely fine. I'll see if Mike can take a little time off and spend it with his instant step granddaughters. Poor guy never had any kids of his own, and now he'll have two step grandchildren. That may come as a shock to him. By the way, he said to tell you hi, and he wanted you to know he was planning on calling you himself with the good news, but duty beckoned, so he asked me to call for him. He said if you have any questions, you can call him tomorrow. Any thoughts on when the wedding's going to be?"

"Yes. Brad met Cash just before we drove up for your wedding, and he asked Cash to be his best man. We're going to wait until Cash finishes his tour of duty in Afghanistan in August, so we're thinking around the middle of September. Mom, I've got a question. I know you've just married Mike, but you know how much I like him. Do you think he'd consider giving me away?"

It was Kelly's turn to cry softly into the phone. "Julia, I can't think of anything that would make both of us happier. I can unequivocally answer yes on his behalf."

"That's great and Mom, I'm planning on you being my maid of honor, and my new stepdaughters will both be flower girls. I know that's a lot of family taking part in a wedding, but hey, it's my wedding, and that's what I want to do. What do you think?"

"I think it will be a perfect wedding, and you're absolutely right, it is your wedding, so don't let anyone try and change your mind. Have it just the way you want it."

"Mom, I need to talk to you about something else. I was going to call you in a day or so, but now is as good as time as ever. I've decided to move in with Brad and the girls. I'm giving up my apartment, so beginning in March, I'll have a new address. I know I'm making the right decision, and it seemed stupid to keep my apartment when I'm spending most of my time with Brad and the girls at his place anyway."

"Julia, that's a decision for you and Brad to make, and it looks like you've already made up your mind, so if that's what you want to do, then I'm very supportive of it."

"That takes a load off of my mind. Even though we've discussed it before, I wasn't really sure how'd you feel about it when the time came. Thanks, Mom."

"I've got another call to make, so I'm going to sign off for now, and don't forget to send those pictures. I can't wait!"

"Love you, Mom, and thanks for everything."

Whew, glad she didn't question me more specifically about what's happening with the investigation. I don't want her to know that I really am concerned Celia will try and do something. I sure don't want to alarm Julia, but in a strange sort of way Celia seems almost crazy to me. Anyway, Julia's got enough on her mind without worrying about me.

CHAPTER TWENTY-THREE

Just as Kelly picked up her cell phone to call Sophie Marchant, it rang while it was in her hand and somewhat startled her. She looked at the screen and saw it was Mike.

"Hi sweetheart. How bad is the fire?"

"About as bad as a fire can be. It's a total loss. The house and everything in it burned to the ground. The wind carried some live embers onto other nearby houses in the area, and some of them caught on fire. The firemen are putting out the last of those fires right now. Fortunately a lot of volunteer firemen showed up, and they were able to put out the small fires that seemed to be everywhere for a time. There's something else you need to know. The fire marshal says it looks like the fire was intentionally set by someone, in other words it was arson. Some state fire investigators are on their way here to see what they can find out about the fire's origin. Given our earlier conversation about Celia, I thought you should know."

"Mike, you don't think Celia did it, do you?"

"At this point, I can't answer yes, and I can't answer no. Fires are not my specialty. I'll wait until the investigators get some evidence, but you know I don't believe in coincidences when it comes to crime. I have a hard time believing Celia just happened to mention to you something about a fire at Sophie's home and then, gee, coincidentally, a fire occurs at her home that very night. Seems way too coincidental to me. Be extra careful until I get home. Don't forget, she said words to you that I consider to be a threat. Make sure you have your gun and Lady with you."

"Lady's with me. I'll get the gun and keep it on me."

"Kelly, I want it in your hand until I get home. Don't forget we know that Celia has access to a .38 caliber pistol, the one taped under the drawer of her nightstand. If she set the fire and then suddenly remembered she told you she thought Sophie's house should be burned down, she might come after you in order to eliminate you as an incriminating witness. I'm going to be tied up here for several more hours, and I sure don't like what I'm thinking. Have you had a chance to call Sophie?"

"No. I'd just picked up the phone to do it when you called. I'll take care of it right now. Poor woman. First Jesse's killed, and then her home's burned down. Now she'll have absolutely no reason to ever come back here. See you later. Be safe."

"You too."

*****

Kelly checked her phone for Sophie's number and called her. It rang several times before it was answered. "Sophie Marchant speaking. May I help you?" she asked.

"Sophie, it's Kelly Reynolds. I'm sorry to bother you this late, but I'm afraid I have some bad news."

"Oh no! Please tell me, what is it?"

"There's been a fire at your home here in Cedar Bay. I don't know much about the details, but Mike is at the scene right now. He just called me and told me that your house and everything in it is a total loss. I'm so sorry."

Sophie was quiet for several moments, and then she said softly, "Kelly, I told you I had been through bad things before. This is a very bad thing, but I will get through it. First Jesse, and now my home with all my beautiful things in it. I guess I wasn't supposed to ever settle down in Cedar Bay. There's nothing for me to go back to now."

"I suppose there's probably not, but you told me earlier today that you have good friends in Portland. You might want to call one of them to be with you tonight."

"A good friend of mine is here now, and he'll help me. Did Mike say what caused the fire? Was it arson?"

It was Kelly's turn to pause and then she said, "Why do you ask?"

"It's probably nothing, but you know how much Jesse's sister hated me. I had gone into The Crush several months ago, and after I entered the store, I heard raised voices coming from the back room. I overheard Celia telling Jesse that I was one of those French foreigners who would ruin Cedar Bay, and he shouldn't have anything to do with me. She said it was her duty as the president of the Historical Society to make sure the city remained pure and protected its historical past. She told him someone should get rid of that monstrosity of a house I'd built on the bluff. I didn't want them to know I had overheard their conversation, so I opened the front door a second time and made a big deal of slamming it. They both came out from the back room, and I pretended that I had just come into the store. Jesse never mentioned the conversation to me. If it was arson, I wonder if Celia is the one who set my house on fire."

"I hate to think of anyone doing something like that, but Mike did tell me arson investigators are going to be investigating the cause of the fire. I'm sure he'll call you as soon as he knows something. Again, I'm so sorry. Good night."

After she ended the call she prepared a dinner plate for Mike with instructions on how to warm it up. She turned on the surface light over the stove to let him know she was in bed and then walked down the hall to the bedroom. She knew that after the fire tonight, tomorrow would be another busy day at the coffee shop, so she'd better get a good night's sleep. She opened the sliding glass door that overlooked the bay and let Lady out. A few minutes later, she realized Lady hadn't come back. She walked over to the door and slid it open. "Lady, come, come in girl," she softly called. A few seconds later, Lady walked through the open door and stood next to Kelly, her hackles up. "What's up, Lady? Did you see a raccoon or a skunk? Easy, girl, it's okay," she said, petting Lady and calming her. "Time for us to go to bed."

I hope it was only a skunk or a raccoon, Kelly thought, her heart pounding in her chest. *I don't know if I'll ever be able to sleep tonight. I'd feel so much better if Mike was home. I don't like being here alone, although technically I'm not alone, because Lady's here with me. What if Celia is out to get me and she's outside? What if Lady heard her or smelled her? Kelly, stop it*, she said to herself. *You've got to get some sleep.*

She got in bed and put her gun on the nightstand. A few minutes later, she was sound asleep. Two hours later she was awakened by Lady standing next to her, a loud growl coming from deep in her throat.

Oh, no. I've never heard Lady growl like that. I don't think I've ever been so scared in my life.

CHAPTER TWENTY-FOUR

Kelly forcefully laid her hand on Lady, sending her a signal to stop growling. She reached for the gun on the nightstand with her other hand, all the while straining her ears to see if she could hear what had caused Lady to growl. She thought she heard soft footsteps and a creak in the wood floor in the hallway. Lady left her side and went around the bed, positioning herself next to the closed door.

It's not my imagination, she thought, *someone is definitely coming down the hall towards my room.* She used every bit of mind focus she had ever learned while taking yoga and meditation classes at the White Cloud Retreat Center to remain calm, willing Lady to be silent and stay where she was. She slid out of bed as quietly as she could, flattened herself on the floor, and then began inching her way under the bed. She could just make out Lady's paws in the darkened room and saw that the dog wasn't moving. *Stay, Lady, stay. Please don't move,* she thought, certain whoever it was in the hallway could hear her heart pounding in her chest. There was no mistaking the sound of footsteps as the person neared the door to her room.

The next thing Kelly knew the door flew open, and a gunshot was fired at the bed, narrowly missing her in her hidden position under the bed. Lady, snarling and barking, leaped at whoever had fired the shot. Kelly heard a strange voice cry out in pain, and then a gun skittered across the wooden floor, landing just outside of her reach. Kelly yelled, "Lady, Guard." She was attempting to inch her way out from underneath the bed when she heard Mike say in a loud commanding voice, "Don't move. Stay where you are. Kelly, are you in here?"

"I'm under the bed. I'm so glad you're here," she said in a shaky voice.

"Rebel, Lady, Guard," Mike said to the two dogs, while he lifted the end of the bed up, allowing Kelly to roll out from under it. She stood up and saw Celia lying on the floor with the two dogs standing over her, keeping her in a prone position. She was holding her arm, and a faint trickle of blood was beginning to show on the sleeve of her blouse where Lady had clamped down on her arm. Mike rolled Celia over and quickly secured her hands in handcuffs behind her back.

"Rebel, Lady, Stand Down. That's all." The quivering dogs walked over to Kelly and Mike, sensing that their masters were no longer in danger. "Kelly, tell me what happened."

She briefly told him what had happened from the time Lady woke her by growling to when he came into the room. Mike got out his phone and called Rich, his chief deputy. "I need you at my house. Now. I have an intruder cuffed, and she shot a bullet into the bed where Kelly had been sleeping just moments earlier, probably thinking Kelly was in it. Luckily Lady alerted her by growling. Kelly heard footsteps coming down the hallway towards the bedroom and managed to hide under the bed. Thankfully the bullet missed her. That's attempted murder for one charge. I'll see what else I can find out."

"Celia, why are you here?" he asked after he'd ended the call.

Something was niggling at Kelly about Celia. She looked Celia up and down, trying to figure out what it was. "Mike, I just remembered something." She walked over to the closet, opened the door, and took her purse from the top shelf.

"Kelly, can't this wait? I'd like to figure out what Celia's doing here and why she just tried to kill you."

"Give me a minute. Yes, here it is." She reached into her purse and took out the small decorative pin from the inside zipper pouch where she'd put it the previous Sunday when she'd found it outside the door of The Crush after she and Mike had discovered Jesse's body. The clasp of the pin had come off of the back of it, but the Arabic numerals "07" were displayed on the pin in small red, white, and blue rhinestones.

"Mike, when I left The Crush with the young deputy who took me home, I found this small pin right outside the door. I picked it up and stuck it in my purse. I'd planned on trying to find something out about it, so I could return it to the owner, but with everything that's happened in the last few days, it slipped my mind. Yesterday, as I told you, Celia came to the coffee shop, and when she was leaving, her purse flew open, and a bunch of things fell out on the floor. When I helped her pick them up, I noticed that a business card of hers had the words 'Cedar Bay Historical Society – Established in 1907' on it. The '07' on her business card was written in a distinctive sort of slanted print, the same way the '07' appears on this pin I found.

"I'm certain the distinctive way the number appears on the pin and the number '07' on her business card are an exact match. I bet if you look in her purse you'll find business cards, and you can see for yourself. Plus, look at her. She's wearing a blouse with a decorative pin on it indicating she's president of The Historical Society, the same number is on the pin, and it's formed by red, white, and blue rhinestones. When I found the pin, it was completely dry. There was no moisture at all on it, yet, it had been foggy and misting earlier that morning. You and I even commented on the way to The Crush how glad we were that the day before, our wedding day, had been sunny and nice, but it was foggy and misting the next day when we discovered Jesse's body. Because the pin was perfectly dry when it should have been covered with moisture, it means it could only have been laying there on the ground for a few minutes. Otherwise it would have been wet from the morning mist.

"I'm certain the pin I found is Celia's pin, and it must have fallen off her blouse, probably as she was rushing out the back door of The Crush. Remember you got a tip from an anonymous witness who said he heard people in the store arguing? I bet it was Celia and Jessie arguing, and somehow during the argument it turned physical, and they began struggling. Jesse must have broken the latch on Celia's pin during that struggle. I'm sure she's the one who killed Jesse. I think the broken pin proves it."

Mike swung his eyes from Kelly to Celia. "Well, Celia, what do you have to say for yourself? You might as well tell me because from what the fire investigators have discovered, it looks like the fire at Sophie Marchant's home was intentionally set. Plus, they've located a gasoline can that was discarded not too far from the fire, and from the quick dusting they did on it for fingerprints, they were pretty sure there would be some on it that they could tie to the fire. I'd be willing to bet they're your fingerprints."

"I'm placing you under arrest. Before you say anything, I'm going to read you your rights." He took a card out of his wallet and began reading Celia her Miranda rights.

"I want a lawyer," she said. "I know I'm entitled to one."

"That you are, but between charges of arson and attempted murder, you might be a lot better off telling me everything, and I could request a more lenient sentence for you if you came clean."

"Mike, excuse me, but I need to talk to Celia." Kelly turned toward Celia and said, "You need to know that Sophie will testify in court that she overheard you tell Jesse, when the two of you were talking in the back room of The Crush, that Sophie's house should be burned down. You'll be seeing that beautiful French woman win a case against you. I can only imagine how that will make you feel. Sophie may have lost Jesse, but ultimately she'll win. Yes, Sophie is going to beat you."

"That's why I killed him," Celia blurted out. "He couldn't help himself when she started sashaying and swishing around him in that high falutin French way. If he'd married her it would have ruined him and the town. I couldn't let him do that. It would tarnish the Allen name to have that hussy carrying it, to say nothing of having more foreigners in Cedar Bay. We don't want or need the likes of her around and we didn't need that house..." She stopped, realizing what she'd said.

"Mike, you told me once you always carry a recorder in your pocket, just in case. Hope this was a just in case time."

"Sweetheart, you've got a good memory. Yes, I recorded all of it. Celia just made a spontaneous and voluntary confession to having killed Jesse and pretty much admitted to having started the fire at Sophie's house. I'm sure she came here to kill you because she realized she'd told you that the house should be burned down, and she was afraid you would connect her with the fire."

"Mike, I'm here," they heard Rich shout out as he opened the front door.

"Come down the hall and into the bedroom. Got someone we need to take to jail. I just got a full confession on the Jesse Allen murder case. I imagine the prints on the gas can that was found out at the site of tonight's big fire will match hers as well, so we can add arson along with the attempted murder of Kelly to the charges."

Rich gasped when he walked into the room and saw Celia Parsons neé Allen handcuffed and sitting on the floor. Involuntarily he said, "Celia, what is going on?" She turned her eyes away from him and began sobbing.

He turned to look at Mike, "I've known Celia since I was a kid. We grew up together, and our families were always very close. Can't tell you how many times I ate dinner at the Allen home. I don't doubt you Mike, but are you sure it's Celia?"

"Yes, in her demented mind, she was determined to keep Cedar Bay pure from outside influences. Unfortunately it involved killing her own brother and probably starting the fire out at the Marchant house tonight. She also tried to kill Kelly, probably in an attempt to cover up her involvement in setting Sophie Marchant's house on fire. See if you can recover the bullet she fired into the bed. Put the bullet and Celia's gun in an evidence bag. I can see it's a .38, and I was told that Celia kept a .38 hidden in her nightstand. Five will get you ten the ballistics tests will also show that the bullet that killed Jesse was fired from that gun. Kelly, you didn't touch the gun, did you?"

"No, if you remember, I was in the embarrassing situation of being stuck under the bed. Thank heavens Lady alerted me, or I don't know what would have happened. By the way, how did you and Rebel know that someone was here, and I was in danger?"

"The light on the hood over the stove wasn't on. We've always had an agreement that you'd turn it on when you went to bed if I had to be out late, so I'd know not to wake you up when I got home. I knew you'd be in bed by now, so the light should have been on. I guess Celia turned it off when she snuck into the house, hoping it might conceal her movements. That was a red flag for me, but before I even noticed that the light wasn't on, Rebel was sniffing the ground like crazy, and as soon as we got to the front door, his body was quivering, and every guard hair he has on his back was up. I knew something was very, very wrong, and I was right. I'm just glad we got here when we did. Rich and I will take Celia to jail and do the necessary paperwork, so I'll be gone for several hours. I'll take Rebel with me, and while I don't expect any problems with Celia, never hurts to have him with me, plus I probably need to give him a couple of special treats."

Lady looked at Kelly with an expectant look on her face. The word "treat" had not gone unnoticed by her.

CHAPTER TWENTY-FIVE

"Well, Mrs. Reynolds, it's been a week now. Are you still glad you agreed to be my wife?" Mike said, pulling Kelly into his arms as they lay in bed, relaxing on Saturday morning.

"I haven't regretted it for a minute, although I didn't expect my first week of marriage to be one where we'd solve a murder, I'd get shot at, or rather the bed where the person thought I was sleeping in got shot at, and I'd find out that I'll be a step grandmother of not one, but two little girls. Wow! This really has been a week to remember. Tell you what. Why don't you relax for a few minutes while I fix a one week special anniversary breakfast for the two of us."

"Sounds good. I'll let the dogs out and get the paper while you start breakfast."

*****

"Kelly, those omelets were fabulous. I like all three meals of the day, but I'd have to say I think breakfast is my favorite," Mike said, as he spread the morning paper out in front of him. Kelly cleared the table, and a few minutes later she heard him gasp.

"Mike, what is it?"

"Remember the guy you followed from the AA meeting, Richard Larson, and the pictures I showed you of his place? Looks like the poor guy just couldn't handle the swings between his alcoholism and trying to get sober. He committed suicide according to this article in the paper. He missed a meeting at his office, and from what the story says, his employer decided he'd had enough, and it was time to fire him. He went out to his house to tell him and found him dead. It was obvious suicide. He left a note saying that the devil alcohol had won. Poor guy."

"If it hadn't been for Celia coming to our house, I probably would have tagged him as the person who killed Jesse. We've been so busy with everything else the last couple of days I don't think you ever told me how Celia's arraignment went."

"Pretty much as expected. She opted for a public defender and pled not guilty to the charge of first degree murder and all the other charges pending against her. If her attorney makes a deal with the district attorney, she might be able to plea bargain to a lesser charge. Rich told me he went to see Mrs. Allen and tell her how sorry he was about Celia. She told him that Sydney had asked her if she could come to live with her. Evidently they were very close, even after the divorce. I remember you telling me that Celia and Sydney were good friends."

"Good grief. Mrs. Allen and Sydney living together? Talk about truth being stranger than fiction! I don't think I've had a chance to tell you that Luke came to the coffee shop yesterday."

"No, you didn't. What did he have to say?"

"He hired a consultant and is committed to making the quality pinot noir that his brother made before his death. Luke told me he'd gone through all of the files Scott had on winemaking and found what he thought was a formula for their best seller. Evidently the consultant agreed that it seemed to be the right recipe for it. Luke also contacted the Pellino brothers and told them in no uncertain terms he was not selling the Center's property, and if he ever found them or any of their employees on his property, he would get a restraining order against them."

"Good for him. Maybe that will get their attention, because it doesn't seem like anything else has. I don't think I've told you I got a call yesterday from the guy who worked for the Pellino Brothers Vineyard."

"No, what did he have to say?"

"He told me he'd overheard Luca telling Dante that he was glad the guy named Guido Salerno wouldn't be returning to the Pellino Brothers Vineyard. Dante said that was good news because he really didn't like the guy. Remember, he was the one I researched who seemed to be a hit man for Angelo Rossi and the Mafia in Chicago. Maybe now things will be a little easier for Luke."

"I hope so. The poor guy's been through so much. I've been meaning to ask you if you'd called Sophie and told her about Celia."

"Yes. I talked to her yesterday, after I received the initial report from the arson investigators. Their report, plus the admission from Celia, is good enough for me. Sophie told me it saddened her to think that Celia would do something like that, but she wasn't surprised. She said she'd already contacted her insurance company, and she expected to receive the funds from the insurance she had on the property within a month or so. She told me she was sorry we'd never met, because she had really liked my wife, meaning you. The lady is a charmer."

"That makes me feel good. I told you I was sure she had nothing to do with Jesse's death. If we can believe everything we've heard, she's a survivor. She's a woman who needs a man, and I'm sure if there's not one in the wings, there will be shortly."

Mike raised one eyebrow and said, "A woman who needs a man? You say that like there's something wrong with a woman needing a man."

"I think you misinterpreted what I said, Sheriff Mike. It's kind of like you needing a little help from me with your investigations. I know I definitely need a man, and I'm just fine with that. Actually, why don't we go back to bed and act like newlyweds?" she said, taking his hand and pulling him out of his chair.

"I think this man can definitely arrange that, Mrs. Reynolds! But I do want you to remember one thing."

"What's that?"

"I'm the sheriff. These are my cases and you just get lucky once in a while. Deal?"

"Deal!"

Rebel and Lady looked at one another, rolled over, and went back to sleep.

RECIPES

KELLY'S QUICHE

Ingredients

8 oz. can refrigerator crescent rolls
2 eggs, slightly beaten
1 cup half and half
1 tbsp. grated Parmesan cheese
1 tbsp. minced onion
Salt and pepper to taste
8 oz. shredded Monterey Jack cheese
1 to 1 1/2 cups cubed cooked meat (I like bacon or ham – if using bacon, crumble it)

Directions

Preheat oven to 400 degrees.

Separate crescent rolls into 8 triangles. Place 5 triangles in a 9" pie pan, pressing together to form a crust, piercing the bottom 6 - 8 times with a fork. Reserve the other 3 triangles for another use. Cut a section of tin foil so that it covers the crust and weight it down with dried beans, rice, or pie weights. Bake 12 minutes until bottom is slightly brown. Let cool.

In a mixing bowl, combine the remaining ingredients and pour the mixture into the crust. Bake for 35-40 minutes until crust is golden brown. Let cool 5 minutes before serving. May be served warm or cold. Enjoy!

BAKED BURRITOS WITH CHICKEN & BEANS (MAKES 6 BURRITOS)

Ingredients

2 ½ cups roasted chicken, shredded
¼ cup green onions, thinly sliced
2 – 3 tbsp. fresh cilantro, chopped
2 medium tomatoes, diced
¼ tsp. ground cumin
1 can (4 ½ oz.) diced green chiles, drained
6 flour tortillas (medium size)
1 can refried beans (can use fat-free to cut calories)
1 cup shredded Mexican cheese blend
1 tbsp. cooking oil
1 cup salsa and 1 avocado, sliced, for garnish

Directions

Preheat oven to 500 degrees. Cover a large baking sheet with aluminum foil.

Combine chicken, green onions, cilantro, tomatoes, cumin, and green chiles in a large mixing bowl, stirring gently to combine.

Place the tortillas on the foil lined cookie sheet and spoon the refried beans evenly on them and then top with the shredded cheese.

Divide the chicken mixture among the tortillas, spooning it down the center of each one. Tightly roll each tortilla and place them seam side down on the foil-covered cookie sheet.

Lightly brush the tops and sides with the oil and bake at 500 degrees for 7 – 10 minutes or until the tortillas starts to get golden brown and crisp. Remove from oven and garnish with salsa and avocado.

Note: I only make as many of these as I know will be eaten. Filling will hold in refrigerator and you can assemble and cook just before serving. Another option is to lower the temperature to 400 degrees, and sprinkle additional cheese over the tops rather than brushing with the oil. Results in a softer burrito. You'll need to cook for about 15 minutes. Enjoy!

NOELLE'S ARTICHOKE & BLUE CHEESE STUFFED PORK CHOPS/WITH SAUCE

Ingredients

2 tbsp. olive oil
2 tbsp. shallots, sliced
1 cup canned artichoke hearts, thinly sliced
1/3 cup blue cheese, crumbled
1 cup Italian seasoned Panko breadcrumbs

Stuffing Directions

Heat the oil in a skillet. Sauté shallots until they become soft and translucent. Add the artichoke hearts and sauté for additional minute. Combine artichoke mixture, blue cheese, and panko breadcrumbs in a bowl. Set aside.

Pork Chop and Sauce Ingredients

4 pork chops (8-10 oz. each)
3 tbsp. olive oil
1 cup grape tomatoes, halved
½ cup red wine
1 cup beef stock
½ cup blue cheese, crumbled
4 tbsp. green onions, sliced

1 tbsp. butter
Parsley for garnish

Pork Chop and Sauce Directions

Preheat oven to 400 degrees.

Using a sharp knife, cut a slit into the side of each pork chop, about 2" long, creating a pocket. Stuff each chop with ¼ of the stuffing previously set aside.

Heat oil in a large skillet over medium heat. Sauté pork chops for 3 minutes on each side. Remove chops from the skillet and place on a baking sheet. Continue cooking chops in oven for 6 – 8 minutes.

Return skillet to the range and over medium heat, add green onions and sauté for 2 minutes. Deglaze pan with red wine for 3 minutes. Add beef stock and cook 2 minutes. Add butter and tomatoes, reduce heat to simmer, and continue cooking 1 – 3 minutes. Add blue cheese and stir until cheese is melted.

Spoon the sauce over the pork chops. Garnish with parsley and serve. Enjoy!

CORA'S RASPBERRY TART

Ingredients

2 eight oz. boxes of fresh raspberries
16 oz. roll of refrigerated plain cookie dough (you'll only need ½ of it)
1 ½ cups whipped cream cheese
1 cup brown sugar
2/3 jar of <u>seedless</u> raspberry jam
Vegetable oil spray, such as Pam
10" or 8" spring form pan

Directions

Preheat oven to 350 degrees.

Cut refrigerated cookie dough package in half. Remove wrapper and bring to room temperature. You can freeze the unused portion.

Place a large sheet of plastic wrap on cutting board. Place cookie dough on plastic sheet and with heel of hand press into a circle about the size of the bottom of the pan. Place second sheet of plastic wrap on top of dough and with a rolling pin, roll out until slightly larger than the size of the pan and about ¼" thick.

Lightly spray bottom and lower inside ¼ of pan. Remove top layer of plastic wrap. With one hand hold bottom section of pan over rolled out dough and slip other hand under bottom layer of plastic dough. Lift and flip onto bottom of pan. Remove remaining layer of plastic wrap. Trim excess dough that may have overlapped the edge of the pan. You can press a small piece of the extra dough into any thin areas, using your thumb and forefinger (helps to dip them in water first). Pinch the dough together along the outside edge to create a small raised ¼" high edge. Fit the spring form over the bottom section of the pan and tighten the spring.

Bake crust for 17 minutes. Remove and place on cooling rack for 30 minutes. After crust has cooled, take a sharp knife and run it around the edges to loosen the crust from the side of the spring form. Once loosened, release the spring form and remove it up and off of the bottom. Using a sharp knife or a cake icing spatula, work it under the crust to free it from the pan bottom. Slide crust onto flat serving dish. (If you have a raised pedestal serving dish, that works well.)

Mix the whipped cream cheese and brown sugar together and stir until consistency of cake icing. Using the back of a teaspoon, spread the mixture evenly over the crust.

Place the fresh raspberries, one at a time, open end down, in a circular pattern starting on the outside edge. Press the berries into the cream cheese mixture until they are firmly fixed in place and touching each other. Continue to make smaller circles of berries until the crust is completely covered.

Pour the raspberry jam into a small bowl and stir until the consistency is smooth. Spoon the jam into the spaces between the berries until the cream cheese mixture is covered. Don't cover the berries.

Place in refrigerator and chill for at least 30 minutes. Cut into pie shaped wedges and serve. Can be prepared in advance. Enjoy!

REUBEN SANDWICH

Ingredients

8 slices rye bread
8 slices deli corned beef
8 slices Swiss cheese
1 cup sauerkraut, drained (I use a colander and press my hand down to get rid of the excess liquid)
2 tbsp. butter, softened
4 tbsp. catsup
4 tbsp. mayonnaise

Directions

Preheat large skillet or griddle on medium heat.

Combine catsup and mayonnaise.

Lightly butter one side of 4 bread slices. Set aside. On the other 4 bread slices evenly spread the catsup mixture then layer 1 slice Swiss cheese, 2 slices corned beef, ¼ cup sauerkraut and second slice of Swiss cheese. Top with the buttered bread slices which have been set aside, buttered sides out. Place assembled sandwiches in skillet or on griddle, buttered sides down. Flip when golden brown on the bottom and cook the other side until it is golden brown. Serve hot.

I love to serve these with big steaming bowls of soup on a cold night. Enjoy!

ABOUT THE AUTHOR

Dianne lives in Huntington Beach, California with her husband Tom, a former California State Senator, and her boxer puppy, Kelly. Her passions are cooking and dogs, so whenever she has a little free time, you can find her in the kitchen or in the back yard throwing a ball for Kelly. She is a frequent contributor to the Huffington Post.

Her other award winning books include:

Kelly's Koffee Shop
Murder at Jade Cove
White Cloud Retreat

Blue Coyote Motel
Coyote in Provence
Cornered Coyote

Website: www.dianneharman.com
Blog: www.dianneharman.com/blog
Email: dianne@dianneharman.com